This book belongs to:

_____

The Misadventures of
Benjamin Bartholomew Piff

1 You Wish

Written and illustrated by
Jason Lethcoe

Grosset & Dunlap

Cover illustration by Kirill Chelushkin

GROSSET & DUNLAP
Published by the Penguin Group
Penguin Group (USA) Inc., 375 Hudson Street, New York, New York 10014, U.S.A.
Penguin Group (Canada), 90 Eglinton Avenue East, Suite 700, Toronto, Ontario,
Canada M4P 2Y3 (a division of Pearson Penguin Canada Inc.)
Penguin Books Ltd, 80 Strand, London WC2R 0RL, England
Penguin Ireland, 25 St Stephen's Green, Dublin 2, Ireland
(a division of Penguin Books Ltd)
Penguin Group (Australia), 250 Camberwell Road, Camberwell, Victoria 3124, Australia
(a division of Pearson Australia Group Pty Ltd)
Penguin Books India Pvt Ltd, 11 Community Centre, Panchsheel Park,
New Delhi—110 017, India
Penguin Group (NZ), Cnr Airborne and Rosedale Roads, Albany, Auckland 1310,
New Zealand (a division of Pearson New Zealand Ltd)
Penguin Books (South Africa) (Pty) Ltd, 24 Sturdee Avenue, Rosebank,
Johannesburg 2196, South Africa

Penguin Books Ltd, Registered Offices:
80 Strand, London WC2R 0RL, England

Library of Congress Cataloging-in-Publication Data

Lethcoe, Jason.
You wish / written and illustrated by Jason Lethcoe ; cover illustration by Kirill Chelushkin.
p. cm. — (The misadventures of Benjamin Bartholomew Piff ; 1)
Summary: When a miserable orphan unknowingly disrupts the balance of power between the
magical realms of wishes and curses, he must join forces with the Wishworks Factory to reclaim
his errant wish and set things right again.
ISBN 978-0-448-44496-3 (hardcover)
[1. Wishes—Fiction. 2. Magic—Fiction. 3. Orphans—Fiction.] I. Title.
PZ7.L56647Yo 2007
[Fic]—dc22
2006018822

10 9 8 7 6 5 4 3 2 1

For my wife, Nancy, who has made all of my wishes come true.

Acknowledgments

I would like to extend special thanks to Trevor Engelson, Nick Osborne, Tara Mark, and Micol Ostow. Thank you for your inspiration and guidance. It is you who have made the incredible journey to Wishworks possible and helped build the Factory.

Star light, star bright,
First star I see tonight,
I wish I may, I wish I might,
Have the wish I wish tonight.

—Nineteenth century American nursery rhyme

TABLE OF CONTENTS

CHAPTER ONE

Benjamin Bartholomew Piff

*B*enjamin Bartholomew Piff scraped out the remains of last week's dinner—a hideous, soupy concoction of clams, spinach, and leftover meatloaf—from inside the immense iron pot. He tried not to retch as he attacked the moldy remains, armed only with a toothbrush. The punishment had been forced upon him by the orphanage chef, who Ben feared and hated more than anyone else: a horrible and greasy old man named Solomon Roach.

"MR. PIFF!" The crusty chef's irritated voice echoed from somewhere above him. Ben stood, his knees dripping with grease and grime, to peer up over the edge of the giant pot.

"Yes, Mr. Roach?"

"When you finish that pot, I have four more that need scrubbing." The gangly cook's black marblelike eyes bore into Ben, a twisted leer curling his upper lip. "I want them all finished by ten o'clock, got it?"

"Yeah, okay."

"What?" Roach's eyes narrowed. "I didn't hear that."

"Yes, Mr. Roach."

Feeling satisfied, the cook grunted his approval and stomped from the room, banging the rusted kitchen door behind him.

Ben looked over to the four humongous remaining pots.

And all because I said I didn't want seconds, Ben thought miserably. Breakfast had consisted of Mr. Roach's usual inedible fare. This morning it was grayish oatmeal topped with boiled beets, and Ben had felt like if he had taken Roach's offer for seconds, he would have thrown up. The consequences for not wanting to eat more of the cook's latest creation was to report to the kitchen and endure three hours of scrubbing, a punishment that was meant to make him a "more grateful and well-mannered boy."

He sighed as he resumed cleaning. It seemed like Mr. Roach was always looking for opportunities to punish him, whether he had done anything wrong or not.

Well, that's all going to change after tonight. Ben grinned as he finished scrubbing the first pot and climbed into the second. He had plotted his escape for weeks, and tonight was the big night. If his plan worked, he would never have to set foot within a thousand miles of a stew pot for the rest of his life.

He finally finished the gruesome job at two minutes to ten, and, without waiting for Mr. Roach to come in and check on his handiwork, he hastily returned the worn toothbrush to the chipped ceramic holder mounted on the wall next to the giant pots. Then, opening an unused bottom drawer inside one of the kitchen cabinets, he removed a small bundled bag that he had hidden earlier.

Ben dashed out the back door of the kitchen and raced through the dead grass of the backyard to his secret hiding spot.

"Hi, Rags," Benjamin greeted the happy terrier as he crawled into the oversize doghouse. He turned the lock he had installed on the doghouse door and, with a small *thud*, set the tightly wrapped bundle on the dirt floor next to the shaggy pup.

As he peered around the inside of the doghouse, Ben allowed himself a small secret smile. His drawings decorated the walls, and a plain, ragged pillow that he had secreted away from his shabby bedroom served as a seat. He plopped down upon it and opened the small package.

Ever since the tragic accident the year before—the airplane crash that had taken his parents away—Benjamin had lived at Pinch's Home for Wayward Boys, a dilapidated orphanage converted from a windowless industrial building that once produced dental tools. Ben hated the place and had good reasons for thinking that it was a joke that it even had the word "home" in its title, for there was nothing about it that felt welcoming at all.

First of all, there was the boys' sleeping quarters. Ben spent his nights in a damp cinder-block room that looked much more like a prison cell than a bedroom, and was filled end to end with rusted army cots. All of the boys at the orphanage slept in the overcrowded room, and there was hardly any space to walk without banging a knee on a piece of furniture or tripping over a pair of shoes that had been left by the edge of someone's cot. It was hot and humid in the summer and ice cold in the winter, and Ben wasn't allowed to hang even a single picture on any of the walls.

Secondly, there was the smell of the place. When Ben first

arrived, the overpowering stench of pine-scented ammonia had assaulted him. He had felt dizzy for days because of the poorly ventilated hallways. He soon discovered that the pine smell masked a much darker, more sinister odor, something like a mountain of mildewed socks that hadn't been washed in months, and which seemed to emanate from some secret place in the building's basement.

Lastly, and most importantly, there were the two people that looked for ways to make his life in the bleak institution as difficult as possible. The first was the head of the orphanage, Ms. Eliza Pinch, a tall, skinny, elderly spinster whose perfume smelled of an old cat box. Why she had ever opened an orphanage was unfathomable to Ben, for she was very vocal about her hatred for children and seemed to harbor a special loathing just for him.

Mr. Roach was the self-appointed "Discipline Master" at the orphanage, and loved nothing more than to dish out punishments to any orphan who looked at him the wrong way. Ben had spent many terrible nights scrubbing the smelly kitchen under Roach's watchful eye, and deeply resented being punished for imagined crimes that he hadn't committed.

Life was certainly a lot different for him now than it had been a year earlier. He'd had a room of his own with a breathtaking view of the mountains, a big television set that could play DVDs and video games . . . and two wonderful parents who loved him more than anything.

Ben would give anything in the whole world to have his parents back for just one day.

Looking down, he opened the bundle and examined what he had smuggled into the doghouse. Twenty dollars in quarters, his savings from helping out Mr. Kunkel, the kindly gardener who had been fired two weeks ago, was shoved inside an old tube sock.

Ms. Pinch regularly searched Ben's possessions, which were kept in an old shoebox underneath his cot. The old woman insisted that the reason for this was simply "routine inspection," but she inspected Ben's box twice as often as the other boys', and Ben suspected that she was hoping to find something that would get him into trouble. Ben had learned from experience that it was in his best interest to hide whatever small valuables he had, or they would mysteriously disappear while being subjected to one of Ms. Pinch's probing searches.

After carefully placing a rusty pocketknife with a broken blade on the ground next to his concealed money, he reached inside the bag and produced his meager food stores. Next to the knife and sock, he set a tin of Vienna sausages and a small foil-wrapped package of frosted Pop-Tarts, both of which he had liberated from the school kitchen two weeks ago during a punishment from Mr. Roach.

He would kill me if he knew. The thought of the greasy cook finding out that he had taken the food filled Ben with sudden dread.

He had a fleeting memory of his first week at the orphanage, when, assuming that he was allowed to eat like he had at home, he had taken a cookie from the chipped jar on the cafeteria counter. The other boys in line had let out a collective gasp when they saw what he had done, and it had taken little time for Ben to realize why they'd reacted with such alarm.

To his surprise and horror, Ben found himself dragged by his ear into the orphanage's filthy kitchen and was roughly forced to climb inside and scrub out Roach's giant blackened stew vats. He soon found out that it was only the first of what would turn out to be almost daily visits to the horrible place.

Later that night, one of the littlest boys at the orphanage, a five-year-old named Shane, brought Ben a small piece of leftover bread that he had saved from his own meal. It was thoughtful, since Ben hadn't been allowed to eat dinner, but his appetite had completely disappeared after spending so much time inside the reeking filth of Roach's pots.

It didn't take long after that first awful week for Ben's thoughts to turn toward planning an escape.

Now, if he could just make it to the bus station tonight without anybody noticing, he would be home free.

He reached into the bag and pulled out the last of his treasures. A small cardboard frame held a photo of a smiling man and woman at the beach. Ben was perched upon his father's shoulders and was grinning happily, his hand raised and holding a gleaming white sand dollar.

He gazed wistfully at the photo, recalling the happy day.

His throat tightening with emotion, he placed the photo back in the bag and gathered up his other things. Rags moved over to the bag and sniffed it curiously.

"Not yet. You can have some sausages when we leave tonight." Ben scratched the hungry puppy behind the ears.

Rags had technically been Mr. Kunkel's dog (the rules at the orphanage were clear about the students not having any pets), but Mr. Kunkel had allowed Ben to secretly care for the puppy, a stray that had wandered onto the school grounds. Rags was Ben's best friend, and, now that Mr. Kunkel was gone, they were together whenever possible. Ben sneaked into the forbidden doghouse for comfort, when he could manage it.

Suddenly the sound of a car engine caught Ben's attention. He peered through the cracked wood of the doghouse at a black Oldsmobile that had pulled through the rusty gates and watched as the car wound its way up the cracked cement driveway to the main entrance of the orphanage.

"Ms. Bloom," he whispered. *I wonder what she's doing here?*

Ben hadn't seen the prim, well-dressed social worker since he had first been admitted to the orphanage. She carried a small package in her arms and, opening the bent screen door, knocked crisply.

A moment later, the lean, hawklike form of Ms. Pinch appeared in the doorway. Ben couldn't make out what was said, but he saw Ms. Pinch nod sourly, then motion vaguely toward the backyard.

I gotta get out of here, Ben thought, glancing around desperately.

He had barely squeezed out of the doghouse door when he heard the raspy shout.

"BENJAMIN PIFF!"

"Coming!" he shouted back, his voice small and uncertain in the summer stillness. He trotted quickly to the front of the house and stood before the two women, trying to look as innocent as possible.

Ms. Bloom smiled down at him and put a hand on his shoulder. "How are things, Ben?"

Ben's eyes flicked to the doorway and caught the warning flash in Ms. Pinch's glare.

"Okay, I guess." Ben cleared his throat awkwardly. Ms. Bloom paused a moment before continuing.

"Good." She adjusted the box that she held in her arms. "I'm sure you're pretty excited about today."

Ben looked up, confused. Ms. Bloom's smile widened and she continued. "You know, turning *eleven*?" She squeezed his shoulder playfully. "Doesn't happen but once in your life, you know?"

The fact that it was Ben's birthday had slipped his mind. It wasn't like he was going to get anything. He forced a smile. "Uh, yeah."

She winked and offered him the box. "I just wanted to check in on you, and, well"—she folded her hands as Ben took the container—"just bring you a little something to celebrate."

Ben caught a whiff of chocolate and peeked underneath the lid. Inside was a small chocolate cake with the words HAPPY BIRTHDAY, BEN written in green frosting on top.

Ben's mouth watered. He hadn't tasted anything good in . . . well, he couldn't remember just how long it had been.

"Well, well, aren't you a lucky boy." Ms. Pinch's eyes flashed dangerously, betraying her falsely sweet voice that rasped from behind the screen door. Ben, momentarily lost in his hunger, remembered his manners.

"Thanks." He beamed a smile at Ms. Bloom. She smiled back and took the keys from her purse.

"You're welcome. I—" Her softened expression was interrupted by the electronic strains of Beethoven's Fifth. She reached into her purse and withdrew a cell phone.

"Yes? Okay. Be right there." Closing the phone, she apologized. "Sorry to cut this short, but I have an urgent case to attend to. Have a really great birthday, Ben." She smiled and gave Ben a final pat on the shoulder before marching briskly to her car.

"Where were you?" Ms. Pinch snapped at Ben as soon as Ms. Bloom was out of earshot. Her eyes narrowed suspiciously as she noticed the dirt on the knees of Ben's jeans. Her voice took on a menacing edge. "You weren't playing with that filthy dog of Kunkel's, were you? I warned you about that last week."

Ben felt his legs turn to water. "No, I wasn't, I was just . . . just playing with my soccer ball."

Ms. Pinch went around to the side of the small house, gazing into the backyard.

"I don't see a ball," she said flatly.

Ben's mind scrambled furiously, searching for an adequate lie.

"I was—I mean—I had just kicked it, and it went over the fence." He flinched nervously as he felt the elderly woman's eyes bear down on him.

"You're not *lying* to me, are you?" She searched his eyes for any sign of dishonesty. Ben stared back, trying to keep his expression as neutral as possible. After an agonizing few moments of this, she stopped, apparently satisfied. Her face took on the expression of familiar dislike.

"Well, I still don't believe you. But whatever you do, you had better keep clear of that *mongrel*. If you set one of your dirty little feet—"

Her speech was interrupted by a sudden commotion at the doghouse door. Ben blanched in terror as he saw Rags, growling and tugging at the handles of Ben's precious bag of belongings that was stuck just inside.

"What in the world?"

Ms. Pinch marched to the doghouse and grabbed the bag from Rags. After rummaging through the contents, her eyes glinted with satisfaction.

"So. It looks like someone was planning on running away." Ben's hands started to shake. He tried to speak, but his mouth was much too dry. Ms. Pinch advanced on him and ripped the cake box out of his arms.

"After all that this school has done for you, this is how you show us gratitude?" Her voice was icy and dangerous. "If you had any idea what the state would do if they found out about this—" She hissed the last part of the sentence and raised her hand as if about to strike. Ben flinched out of habit, but she stopped at the last minute, dropping her arm to her side.

"Get to your room." She pushed him hard, and Ben stumbled inside the entryway. "Mr. Roach will call upon you after supper to help him in the kitchen."

Ben shut the door to the big common room silently behind him and sank onto his army cot. His stomach lurched uncomfortably at the thought of the reeking stew pots he would be scrubbing later. Just thinking about Mr. Roach's smile when he found out that Ben would be his to torture once more made his eyes fill with angry tears and his face feel hot.

"Why did it have to happen?" he whispered through clenched teeth. The tears spilled onto his burning cheeks and splashed warmly down his collar. "Why did my parents have to *die*?"

≈ Chapter Two ≈

Thomas Candlewick, Esq.

"**I** can't believe it. You were here all night again?" Thomas Candlewick lifted his head from his cluttered desk and moaned. "Oh, hi, Perkins. What time is it?"

His assistant, Perkins, squinted through the bottom half of his bifocals to check his wristwatch. "Six forty-five."

Candlewick nodded wearily and stifled a shuddering yawn, then reached up and removed a yellow sticky note that had lodged itself on the side of his stubbly cheek. He gazed at the writing on it with bleary eyes.

INTERNS. 7:00.

He sighed inwardly. If he could just get his hands on a strong cup of coffee, he would be good to go. Perkins shot him an anxious look.

"Thom, are you doing okay? I mean"—Perkins cleared his throat awkwardly—"this is the fourth time this week that you've slept at your desk."

Candlewick gave his portly assistant a tired look. "There're just not enough hours in the day, Perk. The job has to get done. Besides . . ." He yawned hugely. "Unlike you, I don't have a wife and kids waiting for me at home. It's no big deal."

Perkins folded his arms with a smile. "Well, maybe you should start thinking about starting a family. You're not getting any younger, you know."

Candlewick laughed. "Look, I work with kids every day. Why would I *need* any of my own?" He stood up and did his best to straighten his rumpled suit. "Besides, we give them just about anything that they can dream up. Have you ever heard one of them, even once, say 'thank you'?" Candlewick moved to the mirror that hung in the corner behind his desk and fidgeted with his tie.

"Is there any coffee?" he asked.

Perkins nodded and brought a cup from the adjoining office.

Candlewick gulped down the scalding drink and winced.

"Hey, Perk, you want to know *my* deepest wish? I wish that just once you would bring me a cup of coffee that didn't taste like boiled tar."

Perkins rolled his eyes as Candlewick grabbed his hat and strode briskly from the room.

≋ ≋ ≋

Twenty-five minutes later, Candlewick lifted the cover on his ornate pocket watch. The familiar strains of "When You Wish Upon a Star" tinkled gently as the birthday-candle hands ticked toward 7:12 A.M. Candlewick pursed his lips in agitation. Where were the interns? It seemed like no matter how much he stressed the importance of punctuality, they never seemed to get the message. Lifting the dark blue derby perched neatly upon his head, he rubbed a frustrated hand through his mop of prematurely gray hair.

After another thirty-one-and-a-half seconds had passed, the *pit pat* of running footsteps echoed across the cobblestone streets. Huffing and puffing into view, a small group of interns jogged to a stop in front of their new, irritated boss.

Candlewick shut his watch with a *clip* and replaced it into his elegantly striped vest pocket. Perkins, standing behind him, muttered into his ear.

"Not very impressive, are they?"

The corners of Candlewick's mouth twitched in annoyance as he studied the new recruits.

They looked bewildered and exhausted. Most of them wore expressions of stunned amazement. They gaped at the endlessly stretching spectacle in front of them, agog at the glittering spires of the incredible Factory that went as far as the eye could see toward the bright blue horizon.

Unbidden, memories of his own first day at Wishworks rushed into Candlewick's head. He had been nine years old, an orphan with nowhere to go. If it hadn't been for Mr. Snifflewiffle, the kind president of the Factory who had found him sleeping underneath a park bench, who knows where he would have ended up?

He experienced a familiar twist of sadness as he thought back to his lonely childhood. The Snifflewiffles had kindly taken him into their home and raised him as their own son. He had been afraid and suspicious, having spent five days lost in the big city with nothing to eat but the scraps he could scrounge from the trash bins behind restaurants. If he hadn't made that birthday wish . . . the wish that somebody would rescue him . . .

That would have been thirty-one years ago on Friday, Candlewick mused. It was amazing how fast the time went.

One of the interns sneezed, an unusual sound like the skirl of a bagpipe, bringing Candlewick back to the present. The source of the honk was a large purple boy who had no feet, but instead a trail of green smoke where his legs should have been. His golden eyes boggled at the endless spires of the Wishworks Factory. He was accompanied by a purple girl who looked similar but more feminine, with large, pink almond-shaped eyes that matched the tail of smoke trailing beneath her. She smiled broadly, evidently enjoying herself.

I'll have to keep a careful eye on those two, Candlewick thought. They were obviously of Jinn descent, and although the race of Jinns and their magic were largely responsible for powering the Factory, lately many had been disgruntled with the thousand-year-old exclusive agreement they had signed with the company.[1]

The last thing Wishworks needed right now was a labor strike.

Candlewick's thoughts were interrupted by Perkins's tap on his shoulder. He glanced at his assistant, who was now pointing at his wristwatch meaningfully. Candlewick gave

---

[1] The relations between mortals and Jinns have improved over the last fifty years, but there are still many feelings of resentment harbored by the Jinns for having to be confined to a small lamp and enslaved by the human race for centuries.

the little man a perfunctory nod.

"Ladies, gentlemen, Jinns, leprechauns . . ." Candlewick noticed a small fairy who had flitted her way nervously to the front of the crowd. ". . . and fair folk, welcome to the Wishworks Factory." He gestured expansively at the sparkling city towering behind him. The crowd murmured appreciatively.

"We have much to see today, and I know you will have many questions. My name is Mr. Candlewick, and my assistant, Perkins, is now distributing small notebooks for writing down any questions that should pop into your minds as we tour the Factory."

With mumbled thanks, the interns received small leather journals embossed with glittering W's.

"Now, if you will please follow me to the platform on your right, we can get started." Candlewick led the group to a large semicircular platform, above which stretched an unusual machine. Golden gears ticked mechanically, trucking endless rows of exquisitely carved chairs up and down a conveyor belt. Candlewick motioned for some of the closest in the crowd to stand back as he grasped a long lever with a carved walnut handle.

"At *exactly* seven o'clock each morning, you are expected to arrive here at the transportation platform and pull this handle. Doing so will clock you in." He gave them an appraising glance.

"Payroll will be notified if you are tardy three days in a row, so set your alarm clocks tonight." Many of the interns jotted down notes to themselves on this point.

Continuing, Candlewick gestured upward. "This incredible machine is called the Feathered Funicula, and it is the primary mode of transport throughout the Factory." The interns craned their necks at the immensely tall tower surrounded with revolving chairs. With a loud ratcheting sound, Candlewick pulled the lever. One golden chair unhitched itself from the conveyor belt and floated gently to the ground, supported by two fluttering mechanical wings. The time of check-in was magically scribed onto a plaque at the top of the chair.[2]

Candlewick ignored the surprised gasps from the group and held up a hand for silence. "If you will form an orderly line to my left, you may each take a seat. Please don't push any of the buttons or the switches that you will find on the

---

[2] The use of clocks on the chairs was first invented by Wishworks's third president, Wilbur Waffletoffee (1235–1310), and proved to be such an effective tool in reinforcing punctuality that the idea was eventually brought to earth many hundreds of years later, much to the dismay of the average factory worker.

console in front of you, and await my instructions."

The eager crowd pushed forward, and it was some time before Perkins could get them to form an "orderly" line. Soon every intern was seated in a gently hovering chair, waiting for Candlewick to tell him or her what to do next. After settling himself into a velvet-lined chair of his own, Candlewick turned to address the group.

"Okay, everyone ready? Anybody have any problems with motion sickness?"

A small hand went up. It was a pale leprechaun named Nora, who had short green hair.

"Yes?" Candlewick asked.

The tiny girl looked uncomfortable and spoke in a nervous Irish accent. "I don't like to fly, sir. Are you certain these devices of yours are safe?"

Candlewick was quick to assure her that there had not been an accident or mechanical failure with the Feathered Funicula in the last five hundred years, and that she needn't worry about it.[3]

---

[3] The last "accident" occurred in 1541, when Factory worker Pierre de Chaumpinon, after a wild night at the local pub, attempted to be the first employee to fly a Funicula chair to the moon. Witnesses claimed that they lost sight of him after he had ascended about three thousand feet, and his body was never recovered.

Not appearing very relieved, she nervously settled into her seat.

"Now then, you will notice a small button on your right armrest." Several heads turned to the right, searching for the switch. "On my word, please press this button. Do not press the button on the left; that one is the air brake. Once we are in the air, you will hear my voice coming out of the speakers set into the backs of your chairs. Please relax—the initial ascension can be fairly swift." He noticed that the diminutive leprechaun was decidedly pale at this point. Perkins noticed, too, and smiling reassuringly, offered the girl an airsickness bag.

Fizzle, the little fairy that shared the seat next to her, removed a pack of dew- and clover-flavored chewing gum from a glittering satchel and convinced the dubious girl that it would settle her stomach. The leprechaun cautiously took it and, after popping it into her mouth and declaring that it tasted better than it looked, began to work her jaws furiously.

Candlewick pulled an old-fashioned-looking telephone receiver to his mouth. The interns heard his voice crackle over the speakers.

"Is everyone ready? Good. Now . . . here we go. On my count . . . one . . . two . . . three!" To the sound of beating wings, one dozen chairs leaped into the sky, and, with startled shouts and stifled screams, everyone soon floated high above the Factory gates.

ᔌ Chapter Three ᔌ

The Wishworks Factory

Although he had lived and worked at Wishworks for thirty years, Candlewick never got tired of the thrill of flying into work. He smiled as the chair soundlessly approached the gilded roofs of the Factory, each of them reflecting the rosy glow of the morning sun. As the chairs dipped a bit lower for a closer look, he risked a glance behind him to see how the others were faring and chuckled. Most wore expressions of pure exhilaration, but a few, including the leprechaun, who moved her jaws up and down like a jackhammer on the piece of magic gum, held on to the safety bar with white knuckles.

"If you will look below you and to the right, you will see a large domed building. That is the Telepathic Observatory, which houses the largest Thaumaturgic Cardioscope in the world." As Candlewick's voice crackled over the speakers, the interns' faces registered confusion.

Candlewick, having done this tour hundreds of times before, continued. "Now before you jot down the question, 'What is a Thaumaturgic Cardioscope?', I will explain. A Thaumaturgic Cardioscope is a very expensive device that can listen to the dreams and wishes of the human heart. We use it, of course, to tune in to countless individuals on a daily basis and record their deepest desires.[4] These are sorted according to a priority basis, and examined carefully to see that the proper wish protocol has been observed before being sent to the processing plant." Knowing that the pencils behind him were scribbling madly, Candlewick went on. "Take the classic birthday wish, for example. Most people

---

[4] There have been many rumors, often discussed during employee coffee breaks at the Wishworks Factory, about what the actual cost for the Thaumaturgic Cardioscope was. The most popular is that it was purchased from Leonardo da Vinci, who drew up the original blueprints for the scope's design. The legends hold that da Vinci refused to accept money in the transaction, but be granted a wish instead: to paint the world's most famous and valuable masterpiece. The legend goes on to say that he painted the *Mona Lisa* one hour later.

don't get their wishes granted on their birthdays mainly because they haven't followed the specific *rules*."

Candlewick turned the flight control on his chair so that it rotated and hovered in front of his attentive class.

"Number one. The wish must be made with the eyes closed. This insures that the wisher has properly concentrated on the item that they are wishing for. Number two . . ." Candlewick held up two fingers. "Every candle on the cake must be blown out with one breath. Coughing, sputtering, or spitting out the candles doesn't count and will cancel the wish.

"And finally, number three, certainly the most important, and often the reason people blow it." Candlewick shook a warning finger. "The wish must never, *never*, be spoken aloud for anyone else to hear. You don't know how many times we are getting ready to deliver a giant robot or a new pony to some hopeful wisher only to have to turn around and bring it back to the Factory." An intern, a sleepy-looking boy with tousled hair, raised his hand. Candlewick acknowledged him with a nod. "Your name?"

"Pickles, sir, Jonathan . . . *aaaaaah*." The boy stifled a huge yawn. "Jonathan Pickles." The boy blinked slowly. "Sorry, sir. Allergies." He sniffled. "Excuse me, but I don't understand. Doesn't everyone know not to tell anyone what they wished for when they blow out their birthday candles?"

Candlewick smiled sadly. "You know, most kids do. But it's the parents who usually screw it up for them. The child has barely finished making his wish when Mom and Dad start badgering him, 'What did you wish for, Billy? C'mon! You can tell *us*, we won't tell anybody!' And poor Billy, not realizing that he just canceled the wish of a lifetime, tells them."

Candlewick sighed. "If there is one thing I hate to see, it's a good wish ruined by a meddling parent. The rules are very clear. The wisher cannot tell *anybody* what he wished for. Period. There is no time limit on it. Once you tell, *poof*. The wish is canceled."

Then, as if to emphasize the point, Candlewick spun his chair around and pushed a switch on the dashboard, and the group descended toward the Observatory below for a closer look.

The Observatory building didn't resemble a dome as much as a cupcake. Sticking at an odd angle out of its center was something not entirely unlike a telescope, except that it had what looked like a giant brass ear on the end instead of a lens—the Thaumaturgic Cardioscope. The surface of the green dome was covered in slowly moving brass gears. A team of workers, clad in green jumpsuits and matching top

hats, worked tirelessly to oil and polish the machinery. One of them, a man with a handlebar mustache, paused to wave at the group flying a dozen feet above their heads.

Candlewick pulled his watch from his pocket and tapped it with broad gestures, indicating that the man should get back to work. The man smiled good-naturedly and returned to his task.

"As you can see, the clockworks that control the Thaumaturgic Cardioscope must be kept exceptionally clean and oiled. The precision required for the scope to focus in on a single person on an entire planet is quite intricate."

One of the interns, the Jinn girl, raised her hand. "Excuse me, sir?"

Candlewick, about to speak into the receiver once again, stopped and sighed. "Yes? Your name, please?"

The purple girl spoke hesitantly into the microphone mounted on her console. "Jeannie, sir."

Of course. How stupid of me, Candlewick thought. He had forgotten that Jinns didn't go by their given names because they considered them a powerful secret. To all but their most trusted friends, they were known as either "Gene" (the males) or "Jeannie" (the females).

"Your question, Jeannie?"

"Well, sir, I was only wondering. How does the machine

decide which dreams are worth considering and which are not? We Jinns are brought up to believe that any wish must be granted if the human making it masters us."

A fair question, Candlewick thought. He noticed a touch of bitterness in the girl's mention of being mastered by a human. It was a very sensitive subject, and he knew that he would have to be delicate with his reply.

He cleared his throat. "As you are probably aware, part of the Jinn-Wishworks Contract that was signed in 1005 A.D. changed the wish dynamics that Jinns had to abide by for millennia. No longer are Jinns treated as servants. The lamps that once imprisoned all of those of Jinn descent were gathered by the Factory and effectively destroyed.[5]

"All Jinns are now *paid* employees, using their magic to power the Factory. Of course, there are still some Jinn families that are not employees of the Factory at this time, and we are actively recruiting as many as are willing to come and work with us here."

Candlewick, not wanting to get sidetracked in a debate

---

[5] In this, Thomas Candlewick is partly inaccurate. Traditional folklore maintains that a Jinn's lamp can never be destroyed without the use of very specific, powerful magic. There is still hushed debate in some parts of the Wishworks Factory about whether or not the lamps were secretly hidden away because the Factory didn't possess the knowledge or skill to eliminate them.

regarding Jinn/human relations, hurriedly changed the topic. "In terms of who decides which wishes should be granted and which will not, this next department should help you understand that a little better. We will be flying into the Fulfillment department at a fairly low altitude, so please keep your hands and arms inside the chair."

Several interns, who had been enjoying the speedy descent and turns of the chairs, raised their hands above their heads as if on a roller coaster. Upon Candlewick's admonition, they quickly tucked them back inside.

They flew past a tall tower with a giant net on its apex. Candlewick mentioned that the building housed the Dandelion and Falling Star departments. The net gathered all of the dandelion-seed wishes blown up into the sky.

As an aside, he mentioned that unbeknownst to most people, these wishes were not very reliable and only very rarely did any of them come true.[6]

---

[6] When someone makes a wish on a dandelion, the tiny hairs on the dandelion seeds attract the wish and adhere the information to its fluffy fibers. Unfortunately, as any small child can tell you, these tend to fall off quite easily and often don't make it up to the Factory. As far as falling stars go, the problem there lies with the sheer number of wishes made upon seeing one. On average, approximately 10,327 people make wishes for every falling star that is spotted, making it very difficult to sort out whose wishes are whose at the Factory.

One of the interns, the fairy girl, snapped a photo of the huge net as the chairs descended rapidly past it.

Candlewick eased the controls on his chair and followed the line of a bridge that led from the Observatory to a tall slope-roofed building with many windows. The chairs slowed down, and, hovering only a few inches above the ground, entered a tunnel-like doorway.

≈ CHAPTER FOUR ≈
The Fulfillment Department

The Fulfillment building was filled with a mazelike contraption. Factory workers sat all along its multicolored tubular length, staring into view screens. At the start of the machine, two technicians controlled a large screen mounted on a high wall by turning two knobs.

"This first part is where the wish goes through a basic evaluation process. These guys"—Candlewick indicated the technicians—"bring the wish into focus. Watch now; there's one coming in."

A blurry shape rapidly materialized on the screen. A

little boy, perhaps six years old, was poised over a birthday cake, getting ready to blow out his candles. Watching the screen was a bit like watching somebody's home movies. The mother and father stood on either side of the child, having just finished singing "Happy Birthday." The boy blew out the candles and his parents joyfully encouraged him to make a wish. He closed his eyes. Now a new picture began to form: a big yellow toy dump truck. The workers at the console hit a blinking green button and the picture froze.

"Now, this is a pretty typical, everyday birthday wish." Candlewick took out a laser pointer and indicated the toy truck on the screen. He turned to one of the technicians, a pretty brunette. "Delores, please proceed."

"Of course." Delores flashed a smile at Candlewick and pulled a lever. With a whirr of machinery and an electrical hum, a transparent globe approximately the size of a golf ball descended down a chute. At the bottom, Delores picked it up and handed it to Candlewick.

"This," Candlewick said, "is a Wish Globe. Pass it around amongst yourselves." He gave the glowing ball to Gene, the boy Jinn, who examined it and passed it to Jeannie in the chair behind him. "You'll notice that the interior of the glass possesses the imprint of the wish." The interns whispered to each other and pointed at the tiny truck hovering inside the crystal ball. Candlewick paused as the ball was handed back to him.

"The glass ball that you are holding contains a mysterious force of nature, a living entity that we capture and process here at the Factory: one child's birthday wish." Candlewick turned back to Delores and nodded. "Let's see what happens next."

The assembly watched as the screen flickered back to life. After the little boy made his wish, the parents, predictably, asked him what he had wished for. Without hesitation, the unsuspecting boy smiled hugely, revealing two missing front teeth, and said, "A big yellow dump truck!"

An alarm sounded and Candlewick, stuffing the ball into a small container nearby, shouted, "INCOMING!"

Most of the interns reacted quickly, shoving their fingers in their ears or hiding behind their floating chairs. The box that contained the glass globe smoldered and shook violently. Suddenly, with a whistling crescendo, there was an explosion inside of the box like muffled thunder.

The view screen showed the little boy ripping open the box in front of him. To his apparent disappointment, it contained not a dump truck but three pairs of tube socks.

Candlewick winced and handed the smoking package to Delores, who placed it in a bright red garbage can. He thanked her and pushed the throttle, moving the group to the next part of the machine. He cleared his throat and his voice crackled once more over the Funicula loudspeakers.

"So, as you can see, that was very disappointing." The interns' chairs made a sharp right-hand turn, following Candlewick's lead. "Fortunately, some kids do get it right." Candlewick led the interns to a second viewing screen. "This next one happens to be a birthday wish that I personally fulfilled yesterday."

The interns watched as the grinning face of a skinny eight-year-old boy with glasses, wearing a green soccer uniform, materialized on the screen.

"This is Hubert Finklebaum. He made a birthday wish— followed all of the rules to a T, mind you—that he would be the hero of a soccer game his team was playing later that afternoon." Candlewick gave the group a wry grin. "This wasn't easy. Hubert wasn't actually a player on the team. He was the team's mascot." A new picture appeared on the screen. It showed Hubert in a furry costume, having difficulty staying upright due to the mammoth buck-toothed squirrel head on his shoulders.

The interns laughed.

"This footage will give you a good idea of how my department, Kids' Birthday Wishes Ages 3 to 12, handles a challenge like this one." Candlewick motioned for one of the workers to start the film. The lights dimmed, and the interns watched as an elementary-school soccer game commenced.

≋ Chapter Five ≋

Hubert's Soccer Wish

Thomas Candlewick, dressed in a loud Hawaiian shirt and jeans, stood in a throng of enthusiastic parents who were cheering wildly for their sons and daughters on the soccer field. Trying to blend in with the crowd, he nearly collided with a hot-dog vendor as he edged his way closer to the sidelines.

The clock ticked through the last minutes in the second half of the game. The score was tied, 3–3. The interns watched as Candlewick moved to the bench where the coach sat. He tapped the stocky red-faced man on the shoulder. The coach, never taking his eyes off of the game, turned slightly in Candlewick's direction and growled.

"Yeah, yeah, I know. You're wondering why your son is still on the bench. Well, I've only got fifty parents to please, mister. He'll just have to wait his turn."

Candlewick smirked.

"I want you to put Hubert Finklebaum in the game."

The coach whipped his head around like he thought Candlewick was insane. But as he made eye contact with Candlewick, a strange, faraway look came into his eyes. When he spoke, his voice was subdued and distant.

"Yeah. Okay. Hubert. Why not?" Candlewick backed away from the bench as the coach called for a time-out, took his star player out of the game, and replaced him with a very shocked Hubert, who was still wearing the bottom half of his squirrel suit.

There were only thirty seconds to go. Hubert took his place on the field as the whistle blew. The crowd roared! Many parents, just realizing what had happened, shouted angrily at the coach.

Candlewick grinned, enjoying the moment as he studied the field. Suddenly he sniffed loudly and rubbed his nose. The ball, in response to Candlewick's signal, bounced crazily off of one boy's foot and landed directly in front of Hubert.

Hubert looked around wildly for a moment, then began to move the ball downfield.

Several burly boys on the other team rushed for Hubert. Candlewick, covering with his left hand, secretly danced the fingers of his right in several directions. With a jerk, the boys flew out of Hubert's way as if pulled backward on marionette strings. The crowd gasped.

Nothing stood between Hubert and the goal except for the goalie. The seconds ticked down. Five . . . four . . . three . . . two . . . Hubert made an attempt at a kick but slipped on his big squirrel feet and barely touched the ball, falling down on his backside. The ball inched forward. The crowd groaned, thinking that there was no way a ball moving that slowly could make it past the other team's excellent goalie.

With only two seconds on the clock, the ball crept into the goalie's reach. As the boy went to pick it up, however, something strange happened. His hands slipped! Confused, he tried to kick it. His foot slid off of it like butter! Finally, with only a second left, he threw himself on the ground in front of it, but it was no use. The slowest moving ball in the world dragged him into the back of the net.

While the stunned crowd was going wild and a happy Hubert was being hoisted up on the shoulders of his wildly cheering teammates, Candlewick made his way toward a nondescript green outhouse. He took out the magic pocket watch that he used to transport himself to and from the Factory and stepped inside just as a portly man jogged up and grabbed him from behind. Momentarily thrown off guard, Candlewick turned, his expression tense.

"Yes?"

The sweaty man danced in place. "Hey, mister, look, do ya mind if I step in front of ya? I really have to go!" Candlewick relaxed visibly and answered the man.

"I'll only be a minute." And with that, he stepped inside and closed the door. A second later there was a tremendous flash of golden light from behind the outhouse door. And when the portly man opened it cautiously, Candlewick was gone.

There was a moment of black, and then the film continued showing clips of Thomas Candlewick, dressed in many different costumes, fulfilling different children's wishes. He was a clown bringing a little boy his very own baby elephant. Then, he was an ice-cream man emptying a truckload of treats for a dozen excited little girls at a birthday party. Lastly, he was dressed as a pilot, delivering to one little boy his very own jumbo jet airliner.

The interns clapped as the lights came back on. Candlewick waved his hand modestly and smiled. He checked his watch.

"Crikey, where has the time gone?" He addressed the crowd hurriedly. "So you get the general idea of what we do in that situation." He smiled and glanced back up at the screen that once again showed the grinning picture of Hubert. "There is nothing better than making a kid's wish come true." Candlewick waved his thanks to the worker who projected the film and engaged the winged chairs forward.

As they moved along, Nora, the young leprechaun, moved her chair beside Candlewick's. She raised her hand as if to ask a question. Candlewick nodded.

"Sir, I was just wondering if you could answer something for me." The girl fidgeted awkwardly and looked very nervous. In spite of Candlewick's encouraging smile, she still seemed to have difficulty bringing herself to ask her question. Finally, after a long, hesitant pause, she gathered her courage and continued.

"I was just wondering, um, is there such a place as a *curse* factory?" Nora continued hurriedly, "I mean, it was just something I heard about when I was little, you know, something to scare little kids, I guess . . ." She faltered.

Candlewick drew his chair to a halt and gave her a long and searching stare. After a moment he rose from the chair, stepped to the ground, and turned to address the assembled crowd.

"I have just been asked a very interesting question by this young lady here." Candlewick indicated Nora, who blushed and sank low in her seat.

Candlewick scanned the expectant faces in the crowd. "How many of you have heard of a place called *Curseworks*?"

≈ CHAPTER SIX ≈

The Balance of Power

*C*andlewick scanned the anxious faces staring back at him. *Good,* he thought to himself. It was good that they had heard of and had a healthy respect for Wishworks's oldest enemy. Candlewick noticed that Jeannie looked worried and was not surprised when he saw her raise a tentative hand.

"My parents told me that the Curseworks Factory was destroyed fifty years ago," she offered.

Candlewick gave her a comforting smile.

"Yes, it is true that during the time of the Great

Wishworks War, we successfully dismantled most of their curse-enhancing machinery." Candlewick's expression turned grave. "They were terrible devices that were capable of taking ordinary curses and transforming them into monstrous creatures that could attack people in the physical realm." He shifted his gaze to the rest of the group.

"But know this. The Curseworks Factory has since appointed a new leader, a villain named Adolfus Thornblood, and our spies tell us that he has been building a new device from the destroyed machines." Candlewick paused thoughtfully before continuing.

"The ability to make curses has been around since the creation of mankind." The group looked uncomfortable. "Wherever there is pride and arrogance in the human heart, there is also the potential to wish evil on a fellow human being."

Candlewick cleared his throat and continued.

"Simply put, a curse is a wish gone wrong. It is the conscious desire for injustice or harm to happen to someone else who may or may not deserve it. For example," Candlewick explained, "we have all seen people wish for something bad to happen to someone else when they are angry. You don't know how many times I get these from the guys at the Thaumaturgic Cardioscope, telling me that yet another kid has wished that his or her parents were dead, or that the popular person they envy in school would contract some major blood disease." Candlewick held up a handful of black cards with the golden logo of the Cardioscope, an ear enclosed inside of a heart, stamped upon them.[7] The group exchanged concerned whispers. Candlewick went on.

"Fortunately, curses are very difficult to make come true. A wish is always more powerful than a curse."

Gene, the boy Jinn, raised his hand. "Excuse me, but what are the rules with curses? I mean, you explained how wishes work . . ."

"Good question. Well, let's start by comparing the strength of each one." He turned to a nearby worker and, removing one of the small, dark cards from his pocket, spoke to the older man in a low voice. The man nodded, went to a console, and inserted the card into a slot. In moments a recording that showed three men on a golf course materialized.

---

[7] The Curse Cards produced at the Cardioscope serve two purposes. The real purpose is to create a tangible way for the Factory to document the curses that Curseworks receives and attempts to realize on a daily basis. Recently, however, the cards have found a new and separate purpose. They have become highly-prized collectibles to the children of Wishworks employees, who have invented a game called Wish War, and use them in conjunction with Wish Cards to try to outwit their fellow opponents.

"Here is a typical example. Pay attention to the thought balloons that appear above each man's head."

The interns watched as one of the men strode over to the tee and approached a golf ball. As he settled into his stance, a curling, smoky gray balloon materialized above the head of the man standing nearest to him. As it did, the students were surprised to hear the man's thoughts spoken aloud.

"MISS! MISS! I hope he hits it into the lake, the stupid idiot!" The man's face took on a scowling expression. "I hope he pulls a hamstring! That would fix him. Then I could win this game!"

As the words were spoken, the gray balloon morphed and changed. It darkened and turned into something resembling an evil dragon with glowing red eyes. The men, who were oblivious to the smoky beast, continued to watch the first man prepare to hit the ball. Just as the man swung the club in a wide backswing, the dragon made a leap for the man's legs, its jaws open wide.

The club was just about to hit the ball when, quicker than thought, a second balloon appeared above the third man's head, this one white and resembling a knight on horseback. As the knight charged the surprised dragon and knocked it aside with its glittering lance, the man's spoken thought rung out through the air.

"I hope he gets a good shot. He really deserves it; the guy has had a really tough day."

There was a crack as the first man made impact with the golf ball and hit an amazing drive down the fairway. The third man beamed at his friend and complimented him on his shot, while the man who had made the curse fumed and scowled as he hoisted his golf bag on his shoulder.

Candlewick nodded at the worker and the image froze and disappeared. "Wishes and curses happen every day. These are very different than a child's birthday wishes. No rules are necessary because they have far less power. For every curse somebody wants to happen, someone else is usually there to wish good things, thoughts, or feelings for the person and cancels it out."

Nora raised her hand. "Yes?" asked Candlewick.

"So when a child wishes his parents were dead, or that the teacher at school would fall off a cliff, that curse can be countered by anyone who loves the teacher or the parents and wishes kindness toward them?"

Candlewick chuckled. "In some cases, when I've got somebody that's a real stinker, sometimes all that they have is their mother's love. But make no mistake . . ." Candlewick's eyes twinkled. "A mother's evening prayers for her child are one of the most powerful curse-fighters in the world."

Perkins, who had been hovering nearby, maneuvered his chair to Candlewick's side and handed him a note. Candlewick scanned it briefly, nodded, then turned back to his rapt audience.

"But, this is where Curseworks comes into the picture. Adolfus Thornblood, the head of the Curseworks Factory, has spent his life trying to find a way to make curses stronger than wishes. He would like nothing more than to eliminate the hopes and dreams of mankind and replace them with evil curses."

An uncomfortable, heavy silence filled the chamber, but was broken when a small dinging bell went off. Candlewick reached into his pocket and took out a golden cell phone.

"Yes?" He removed his pocket watch from his vest and checked it. "Okay, I'll be right up." He motioned for Perkins to move his chair in front of the interns.

"Perkins here will take you through the rest of the tour." He thumped the meaty shoulders of his assistant affectionately, then smiled at the concerned interns. "And remember, a good wish is always stronger than the worst curse."

As Candlewick tipped his hat and was about to leave, he felt one of the interns tap him on the shoulder. He turned to see Jeannie and Nora behind him, looking awkward. The

Jinn nudged the leprechaun, indicating that she should speak. Nora cleared her throat.

"Um, we just wanted to say that if you should ever need volunteers to help defend the Factory or anything . . ." Nora blushed, turning a bright shade of green.

Candlewick smiled. "You got it. You're Jeannie and Nora, right?" The two nodded. He made a quick note of their names in his book. "I'll have you assigned to a special department that will begin training you in wish troubleshooting." He shut the notebook and replaced it in his pocket. "Sometimes the biggest threat to the Factory is when a wish goes wrong."

He looked pointedly at Jeannie and addressed her in low tones so that the other interns wouldn't overhear. "Thank you for volunteering. We always appreciate having another Jinn at Wishworks."

Jeannie nodded and smiled grimly. "No problem."

Candlewick grinned, and then, turning back to the assembled chairs, gave the interns a quick wave and strode from the room.

CHAPTER SEVEN

The Boardroom

Candlewick trotted two at a time up the red-carpeted winding staircase that led to the massive offices of the president of Wishworks, Leo Snifflewiffle, who also happened to be Candlewick's stepfather. When he arrived at the massive wooden doors, Candlewick paused to straighten his tie and then, taking a deep breath, strode boldly into the room.

Snifflewiffle's bespectacled assistant, Cherie, was busily sorting through countless black and golden cards that had recently arrived from the Thaumaturgic Cardioscope. When she heard the door close, she glanced up and smiled.

"Hi, Thom. They're waiting for you in the boardroom."

"Well, this is it, Cherie," Candlewick said. "I can't believe today is the day they're finally going to decide."

Cherie paused in her sorting of the cards and gave Candlewick an encouraging grin. "Good luck. You really deserve it."

"Thanks."

Candlewick walked to the second set of towering golden doors, carved with intricate designs. He turned the ornate handles and the doors swung open to reveal the massive boardroom, which he always thought resembled King Arthur's Round Table.

Seated around the table were the fifty board members, each in his or her own thronelike chair.

President Snifflewiffle sat at the head of the table in the largest throne and was boosted to a position where he could see over the tabletop by several velvet cushions piled on top of one another. He was a short man, well into his seventies, but his round, unlined face and naturally jet-black hair made him look much younger.

Candlewick made his way around the room, shaking everyone's hands. Seated next to Snifflewiffle was a younger man, near in age to Candlewick himself. Candlewick's stomach turned at the thought of making contact with his longtime adversary—who happened also to be his stepbrother. Simon Spinchley Snifflewiffle was a handsome man with very white teeth. He smiled often but had the kind of smile that never reached his eyes, which were close-set and unusually small.

When they were children, Candlewick and his step-brother had once been friends. They used to have fun exploring the Factory together, but those days were long past. Ever since Simon had been promoted to head up the Falling Star department, he and Candlewick had been competing for the eventual presidency of Wishworks. Candlewick hated the way Simon tried to undermine him to his stepfather, who seemed oblivious to Simon's tactics.

After exchanging forced smiles with Simon, Candlewick took his seat on the other side of his stepfather's massive throne. The doors in the back of the room opened and two interns strode in, carrying a large silver tray of butter cookies and steaming mugs of hot chocolate.[8] This was Snifflewiffle's

---

[8] Leo Snifflewiffle's love for hot chocolate was so legendary that he kept a Chocolate Moose in the Jacuzzi behind his house. This very rare breed (for which the dessert was later named) produces the finest-tasting chocolate milk in the world. When milked after spending several relaxing hours in a hot Jacuzzi, the hot chocolate that results is also the best in the world.

usual boardroom snack, and the little man looked to the tray with childlike eagerness as the young people placed cups and cookies in front of each member. After everyone had been served, the largest cup, a big silver mug embossed with a golden "S," was placed in Snifflewiffle's hands. His joyful expression, however, quickly faded as he stared down into the cup.

"Hey, there are only two marshmallows in mine." Snifflewiffle's lower lip protruded. One of the interns quickly apologized and rushed from the room, reappearing almost instantly with a small crystal bowl filled to the top with fluffy white marshmallows.

"Thank you." Snifflewiffle beamed at the youth, who smiled back awkwardly. After taking a sip of the melted chocolate, the president turned his attention back to the assembled members. His small voice piped up shrilly, sounding very much like the toot of a tin whistle.

"Well, let's just get right down to it, shall we?" Snifflewiffle's eyes twinkled as he took in the expectant faces. "Today is the day we announce the new president of the Factory."

Candlewick held his breath as the boardroom erupted into murmurs and nods. He shot a quick glance at Simon, who shot him back a smug and confident look. *I'll bet he did something,* Candlewick mused bitterly. *If I were a cursing man, I can't think of anyone who would deserve one more . . .*

Snifflewiffle munched a bite of cookie and then continued his speech. "Obviously, Thom and Simon are aware of the magnitude and difficulty of this decision. I have been president of the Factory for more years than I can count and am looking forward to retirement." He grinned impishly and whispered loudly, "Mrs. Snifflewiffle and I have our bags packed and are ready to leave for a place on earth—Hawaii, actually—this very afternoon." The board members smiled and clapped politely for Snifflewiffle, who waved modestly.

"I have enjoyed my time as president immensely and am happy to leave the Factory in very capable hands. The person we have elected has exhibited the extraordinary qualities that go into making a great leader, as well as running his particular department with unflagging dedication." Candlewick's heart pumped wildly.

Snifflewiffle continued. "So it is with a great sense of fatherly pride that I announce that, from this moment, henceforth, your new president will be . . ."

Suddenly a loud *whoop* split the air. The boardroom erupted into mass confusion. A harried Perkins burst through the doors and, huffing and wheezing, ran to the seat where Candlewick was sitting. Candlewick stood and addressed his pale, breathless assistant.

"What's the matter?"

Perkins wiped the sweat from his forehead. The grizzled members of the board fidgeted nervously, and Candlewick noticed that even Simon appeared to be taken off guard.

Perkins's voice shook with emotion. "Thom." Perkins rested a quivering hand on the heavy tabletop. "It has finally happened."

⪻ CHAPTER EIGHT ⪼

The Wish That Changed Everything

Benjamin stared at the smoking candle with a sad smile. *What does it matter, anyway?* he thought. *Wishes never really come true.*

The hands on the clock in the deserted kitchen moved to twelve midnight. Ben had finally finished scrubbing out the enormous stew pots and was now covered head to toe with the dripping, smelly remains of Mr. Roach's chili, a concoction of what many students speculated was the discarded leftovers from the last six weeks.

When he had arrived in the kitchen after dinner, Ben had

had to endure a tirade of countless insults from Mr. Roach about his apparent "lack of gratitude to the orphanage" and his "obstinate and willful disobedience." Then, to Ben's dismay, the scrawny cook had triumphantly revealed the confiscated birthday cake Ms. Bloom had brought and, with much relish, proceeded to lock it inside the rusty refrigerator.

Ben had ignored the grating laughter, pretending to be engrossed in selecting one of the green toothbrushes that the cook kept for scrubbing the pots. When Mr. Roach believed Ben's back was turned, he had hidden the key inside of a drawer, a fact that Ben noted while studying the cook's reflection in one of the battered toasters that littered the grimy, tiled countertop. After he'd waited long enough for Mr. Roach to return to his quarters, it had taken Ben no time to liberate his only birthday present, cut a large slice of the gooey cake, and light a candle for himself.

Ben glanced at the small black wick of the burned-out candle and sighed. *What a lousy birthday.*

Suddenly a voice that sounded like nails on a chalkboard startled him out of his morose thoughts.

"What did you wish for, Ben?"

Mr. Roach, in his pajamas and tattered bathrobe, stood in the darkened hallway with his hands crossed over his wrinkled and wiry frame. His black, beetled eyes glinted with

triumphant glee. Ben knew that this time the punishment would be far worse than a long lecture from Ms. Pinch or an evening of scrubbing stew pots. He gulped and replied in as steady a whisper as he could manage.

"Nothing."

Mr. Roach approached, winding his way around the kitchen table like a slithering snake, baring his crooked, yellow teeth.

"Oh, I'm sure it was *something*."

He was only several inches taller than Ben but seemed to tower over him, staring down with an evil smile. "Tell me."

Ben was sick with fear. He had been tormented by Mr. Roach long enough to know that the evil cook would never rest until Ben did what he asked. But even though he was scared out of his skin, he couldn't bring himself to confess what he had wished for. Ben hadn't been too serious when he made the wish, figuring he might as well make it for something outrageous. But without really realizing it, maybe, just maybe, there was a tiny place deep inside of him that *wanted* to believe that such a wish were possible.

Feeling desperate, he wanted something to happen more than anything else he had wanted in a long time.

I wish Mr. Roach would forget about this whole thing and go back to bed.

A strange, faraway look transformed the cook's features. He stepped back a few paces, looking surprised. Then, with his mouth gaping hugely, he yawned. His eyes were bloodshot and heavy. Mumbling as he turned to go back down the hallway, Ben heard him say, "Musta been a bad dream." And without even closing the kitchen door behind him, Mr. Roach tramped upstairs to his tiny stone room and collapsed onto his rumpled sheets, snoring loudly.

Ben was stunned. He felt dizzy and sat down on a kitchen chair so that his legs wouldn't give way beneath him. *Did that really just happen?* He gazed around the darkened kitchen for several moments, his mind racing, as he listened to the tick of the clock on the wall.

It may have just been a coincidence. He was probably really tired or something. In spite of the logic of this thought, Ben sensed that it couldn't be true. Mr. Roach had reacted too strangely when Ben had made the wish for him to go back to bed. But since when did birthday wishes come true? He had made them all of his life, and up until this point they had never happened.

He glanced down at the front of his oily, grime-encrusted shirt. Staring at it, he mumbled, "I wish I had some different clothes on."

The shirt seemed to evaporate in a blurry haze, and,

before Ben realized what was happening, a brand-new clean black T-shirt was in its place.

Whoa.

Heart thumping, Ben walked over to the box that contained the only evidence that he had been in the forbidden kitchen. He eyed the partly eaten birthday cake and concentrated.

I wish the cake was whole again and nobody could tell that I had eaten any.

There was a brief pause. Then, like a film played backward, tiny crumbs of cake rapidly began to fill in the missing wedge. In moments the cake was restored to its original condition. Eyes boggling, Ben noticed that even the chunk of frosting with the words "Happy Birthday" written upon it was perfectly restored.

Oh, man. The world spun crazily around Ben as he stumbled out into the warm summer night and made his way back to his army cot in the dormitory.

My wish for unlimited wishes has come true!

≋ CHAPTER NINE ≋

Unlimited Wishes

*C*andlewick stared at the huge clock, which occupied an entire plate-glass window outside of the richly paneled boardroom. *Six hours.* The kid had lasted six hours without bragging to anybody after making the wish that could ruin everything. It was unheard of! And here it was, on the day Candlewick finally got the job that he had worked for, sweated over, and dreamed of since he had started at the Factory!

The kid will crack. They always do, he reassured himself.

Candlewick gazed off the balcony down to the Factory

floor below. The mood was anxious as the workers watched clips of the boy who had made the wish: Benjamin Bartholomew Piff.

Memories of his early days at the Factory, when he had spent countless hours in the library memorizing the names of past Wishworks presidents, came rushing back to Candlewick. As a young boy he had been fascinated by the unusual names and personalities that were printed on each page of the gold-edged tome labeled *Wishworks Presidents, Past to Present*. To him, the presidents were larger than life, incredible heroes.

Bubbdouble, Pfefferminz, Waffletoffee, Hairyhead . . .

He recited the familiar names to himself as he stared off into space.

Snooplewhoop . . . founder of the Everlasting Circus . . . Rumbleroot, Pokenose, Warblegrunt . . . He united the Jinns and destroyed the lamps . . . "Lucky Penny" Thicklepick . . . Cheeseweasle . . . Snifflewiffle . . .

He paused, swallowing hard before whispering the last name in the list to himself.

"Candlewick."

Two technicians clothed in green jumpsuits with silver winged Wishworks logos on their breast pockets approached Candlewick, interrupting his thoughts.

"Sir, you sent for us?"

Candlewick jumped and spoke to the nearest technician. "Yeah. I need you guys to go over to the Thaumaturgic Cardioscope and tell them that I want them to send over all they have on this kid. I want to know every single birthday wish that Benjamin Bartholomew Piff has made for the last ten years, understand?"

"We're on it." The first technician nodded and motioned for her partner to follow. Candlewick sighed and ran a frustrated hand through his hair. *I gotta find out what makes this kid tick.*

When Snifflewiffle had announced that Candlewick would be Wishworks's next president, Candlewick had been surprised by his stepbrother's reaction. He'd expected something other than the warm smile and congratulatory handshake that Simon offered him.

Maybe it was because he wouldn't have wanted his first day as president to be filled with a problem like this one, Candlewick thought bitterly.

Well, whatever he did, he wouldn't let on that he was concerned. He couldn't show any of his anxiety to the board members—not on his first day as president. Besides, in the past, other kids had tried a stunt like this one. They *always* ended up telling somebody about it and canceling the wish.

"Thom, you do realize that if this goes on much longer, we are going to have to do something." Candlewick turned and looked down at his stepfather, who had joined him on the balcony.

"I thought you were going to Hawaii?"

Snifflewiffle shrugged. "I postponed the trip. I thought you might need me around a little longer."

Candlewick smiled gratefully. "Thanks, Dad, but you didn't have to do that. I think I can handle it. It shouldn't be a problem." Candlewick looked back up at the mammoth second hand rotating on the clock. "I'm sure the kid will tell somebody any minute now."

Snifflewiffle sighed. "I'm not so sure, Thom. It's going on seven hours and he hasn't told a soul." Snifflewiffle removed his round spectacles and rubbed a hand across his tired eyes. "You know the rules. Each child is allowed only one birthday wish; any more and the Factory has to take away other kids' wishes to compensate for the stolen ones."

Candlewick knew. He had seen a kid make a similar wish once, a wish for a million wishes. They had all held their breath as they watched the kid get through half a dozen of them before finally boasting about it to his friends. But it had been terrible to watch a little girl in Russia have the unicorn of her dreams suddenly fall into the mud and vanish beneath her mid-gallop, not to mention the other five kids around the world whose deepest wishes were suddenly gone—all because of that kid and his greedy wish.[9]

"I have ordered that Benjamin's Wish Globe be locked up in the vault. It is far too dangerous to have something of that power lying around. If the wrong person got their hands on it . . ." Snifflewiffle's piping voice trailed off.

Candlewick knew exactly what he meant. Although employees at the Factory understood that stealing a human wish was forbidden, this one might be too tempting to resist.

"Dad, would you mind calling the Eradicators[10] for me? There are a couple of interns I just sent over there for training who might be able to help me out on this one." He gave Snifflewiffle the notebook with Jeannie and Nora's names. "I'll get the kid to crack, I promise." Candlewick picked up his golden phone and dialed a number.

---

[9] It had only been a few days before that Candlewick mentioned a girl in Edinburgh, Scotland, who had wished for "everything in the world." Besides the usual complications that arise from a wish of that nature, the second biggest problem the Factory faced was to find enough boxes to fulfill the wish! Fortunately, the girl told her best friend ten minutes later and canceled the wish.

[10] An elite team of troubleshooters, the Eradicators take care of most wish-related catastrophes at the Factory.

"Hi, Thom," Perkins answered.

"Hey, Perk. Listen, could you hold my calls for a little while? I'm going to go down and take care of the situation myself. Oh, and also, if you could, arrange for transportation to depart from the Funicula in five minutes."

"You got it, boss."

Snifflewiffle gave his son a reassuring smile. "You can handle this, son. I know you can. We're all counting on you."

Candlewick smiled back with more confidence than he actually felt. "Don't worry, Dad. I won't let you down."

⁓ CHAPTER TEN ⁓

A Few Changes

"Will there be anything else, sir?"

"Yes, I think so." Ben sipped the last of his fresh-squeezed lemonade. Mr. Roach, dressed in a waiter's uniform, stood next to him, smiling expectantly. Ben looked over at the long line of boys, all holding empty bowls and staring at him with awestruck expressions.

"Another round of ice cream." Ben glanced over at the boy nearest to him, a thin, ragged-looking five-year-old. "What do you think, Shane, more pistachio?" The little boy nodded his head in disbelief. Ben turned to Mr. Roach. "Pistachio, if you please, Mr. Roach. But this time bring everybody his own carton." Ben looked down and winked at Shane. "We're barely getting started."

Mr. Roach jumped to attention. "Right away, sir." He was off at a trot, carrying Ben's empty lemonade glass and several dozen bowls on a large tray. Ben swung a leg over the side of his hammock and adjusted his sunglasses. The changes he'd made at Pinch's Home for Wayward Boys were definitely an improvement. He glanced to his left, where Rags lay stretched out on his back, legs in the air and a tiny matching pair of sunglasses perched upon his doggy nose.

"This is the life, huh, Rags?"

The dog gave Ben a lazy look and shot out his pink tongue in approval. Ben grinned, looked at his watch, and glanced up at the other boys crowded around him.

"Everybody having a good time?"

There were various shouts of approval from the boys gathered around Ben's hammock.

Happy murmurs spread through the crowd as a blue truck covered with stickers pulled into the orphanage's driveway. Mr. Roach strode to the truck and returned carrying half-gallon cartons of pistachio ice cream. He quickly distributed them to the cheering crowd.

Seconds later, Ms. Pinch ran to greet another delivery

truck, her spindly legs pumping furiously. She breathlessly instructed several brown-uniformed deliverymen carrying large cardboard boxes to hurry over to where Ben and the assembled throng of boys waited.

"What took them so long to get here?" Ben demanded.

Ms. Pinch looked stricken with fear. She shot Mr. Roach an anxious glance and then, mustering her courage, spoke up.

"I'm so sorry, dear, but it took the engravers all afternoon to customize every Playstation." Ben, ignoring Ms. Pinch, hopped down from his hammock, took a box addressed to himself, and opened it. The glittering gold-plated Playstation, along with two controllers etched with BEN and RAGS, made him grin from ear to ear. When Ms. Pinch saw that he was pleased, she visibly relaxed.

"Very nice. Very nice. Now all we need are . . ." Ben looked around for a moment, then focused on the delivery truck in the driveway. He whispered something under his breath. Then he turned to the nearest deliveryman with a strange expression on his face. "Uh, didn't you forget something?"

The balding man scratched his head and looked at Ben, momentarily confused, then checked the packing list on his clipboard.

"No, I don't think there was anything else . . ." He rifled

through the pink, crinkly pages. "Wait a sec. My bad. Wow, how did I miss that? I'm sure it wasn't there before . . ." Ben chuckled with private pleasure as the man called to his coworkers to unload the rest of the delivery.

Moments later the men returned, struggling under the load of fifty flat-screen television sets and a massive outdoor power generator.

"Sweet!" Ben shouted gleefully as he plugged a TV into the generator and turned on his new Playstation. The other boys, upon realizing that Ben had ordered customized game consoles and televisions for them as well, let out a loud cheer and hurriedly began unpacking their presents. Shane was so overcome with emotion that he just sat with the unopened Playstation box on his lap, wiping tears from his eyes with his tiny, grubby fist.

Suddenly, a third truck screeched to a stop in the driveway. Ben looked up from his favorite game, Outback Hunter, and noticed that the van had a large Channel 15 News logo on its side.

A pretty reporter and a camera crew spotted Ben and strode briskly to where he stood.

"You must be Ben! Come on, guys, let's get a shot of this." She motioned for the crew to surround Ben. A middle-aged woman wearing large glasses checked the reporter's makeup, and after a quick powder, the newswoman gripped a microphone in her hand as she addressed the camera.

"I'm Carla Schaeffer, and we are coming to you live from Pinch's Home for Wayward Boys where we are meeting Benjamin Piff, the luckiest kid in Newbury Park, California."

"Tell us all about it, Ben," Carla said, thrusting the microphone in front of him. "How did this sudden good fortune happen to you? Did you win the lottery or something?"

She smiled prettily.

Ben, taken off guard, replied, "Um, no. It was my birthday."

Carla smiled, crinkling her nose. "Your *birthday*? Well, isn't that just great?" She batted her eyelashes, and Ben felt himself blush.

"Well, Ben, it looks to me like the people who run this orphanage must love you a whole lot to give you such great stuff on your birthday."

Ben scowled, and without thinking, replied, "No. The reason I have all this stuff is because I made a wi—"

Ben stopped, noticing the eager expression in the newswoman's eyes. What was going on here? Why did these people show up wanting to know about his birthday?

Carla pressed in closer to Ben. "I'm sorry, sweetie, we didn't get that. What was it you were saying? That you made a birthday . . ."

She let the question hang there. Ben clamped his lips shut. Something was really fishy here, and although he didn't know exactly what was going on, some inner voice told him that he shouldn't say any more.

Carla laughed nervously, motioned for the camera to keep running, and pointed the microphone again in Ben's face.

"C'mon, sweetie. There are millions of people watching. Don't you want to let the world know how such a clever and resourceful boy like yourself got all of this cool stuff for his birthday?"

Ben looked at the camera. *Millions of people?* He thought of everyone glued to their television sets, wondering why he was standing there saying nothing. He didn't want to look completely stupid.

He cleared his throat. What could it hurt? After shifting awkwardly on his feet, he gazed at the camera and opened his mouth to speak.

"I . . ."

But the words died in his throat. He gazed at the news van parked in the driveway.

"There is no channel fifteen." He spoke softly, feeling a little confused, then gave Carla a sharp glance. "Hey, who are you guys, anyway?" He stood up.

Carla smiled nervously and took a few hesitant steps back. "Umm, we're a very small station, a, umm, a local, syndicated thingy . . ."

Ben was unconvinced. Carla, walking backward, didn't see the extension cord that stretched from the power generator into the house. With a small yelp, she tripped and fell, landing on the grass with her feet in the air. As she did, to Ben's shock and surprise, he saw her legs turn into pinkish smoke!

"What the . . ."

But he didn't have time to finish his sentence. The crew hoisted Carla to her feet, scrambled into the news van, and squealed down the driveway.

≋ ≋ ≋

Inside the speeding van the cameraman whipped off his baseball cap, sunglasses, and goatee, revealing Thomas Candlewick's exasperated face. He turned to Carla and her makeup lady, who looked harried and disappointed. Their forms began to melt. In moments, sitting in their places were Jeannie and Nora, the Jinn and leprechaun who Candlewick had shown around the Factory only a day before. They squirmed uncomfortably.

"I didn't know he would be so tough." Jeannie frowned, her pink smoky tail turning an agitated shade of crimson.

"Yeah, he saw right through it." Candlewick paused a moment, his brow knitted. After a few moments of silence, he sighed. "He's way too sharp. The disguises won't work a second time."

Jeannie looked concerned. "What do you think we should do?"

Candlewick paused before answering.

"We have no time to lose. I think we're going to have to come clean." His expression was grim as he picked up the two-way radio.

"Hi, Cherie, it's Thom. Is my dad around?"

≋ CHAPTER ELEVEN ≋

Simon S. Snifflewiffle

*I*t had been easy to take advantage of the old man's trust. When Candlewick left in his big hurry to get down to earth and deal with the crisis, Simon had simply stepped in and offered his help.

Idiot. Simon knew that Snifflewiffle had always wanted his stepbrother to have the position. Simon's initial plan had been to bide his time, and after Candlewick had gotten the promotion, he would appear to be happy to take on the role of vice president. Then, after Candlewick had enjoyed a few weeks in office, Simon would arrange for the unfortunate accident that he had been planning for years.

Simon thought back to a time long past, when he and Candlewick were children. Candlewick had been a grateful, good-hearted boy who always had his father's praise and admiration. Simon had grown up resenting being constantly told to be "more like his brother."

The years went by, and Simon harbored secret, jealous thoughts that festered and grew until the hate he felt for his brother eventually turned murderous. Until now, he had only fantasized about Candlewick's demise, but the arrival of this incredible stroke of fortune changed everything. Now he would be able to accomplish his plans even more quickly. He knew just the person who could make all of the curses he had ever wished upon his brother come true.

His fingers stroked the glowing crystal globe resting in his velvet-lined coat pocket, and he allowed himself a secret smile.

His stupid, trusting father had even given him the keys to the vault! It was too hilarious to believe! He'd been handed his future and hadn't had to kill a single soul to get it.

Striding boldly past the guards at the massive gates and out to the cobblestone streets that led to the Feathered Funicula, Simon Spinchley Snifflewiffle whistled a happy tune through his very white teeth.

≈ CHAPTER TWELVE ≈
Coming Clean

"**D**ad, the kid knows something is up," Candlewick said into the two-way radio.

Nora sat in the backseat of the Wishworks surveillance vehicle and nudged Jeannie, whispering softly.

"I don't know about this. We've never revealed ourselves to mortals before."

Jeannie, not wanting to disturb the intense conversation between Candlewick and his stepfather, moved into the backseat to continue the conversation.

"Yes, but this time it is different. The human child senses

that he has accomplished something extraordinary, and he doesn't want to let it go." She glanced at Candlewick, then turned back to Nora, looking concerned.

"Besides, who knows how many children have lost their wishes already? It's been ten hours since he made the wish, and he certainly has been busy."

Nora nodded in agreement. "I know that if we don't stop him he could bring down the entire Factory. But in a way"— she offered Jeannie a lopsided grin—"you can't really blame him, can you? I mean, he did pull it off, and I don't think anybody has ever done that before."

Jeannie scowled. "Humans are all the same. They only think about themselves."

". . . all I can do is let him know the gravity of the situation and hope he makes the right choice," the interns heard Candlewick say.

Leo Snifflewiffle's voice crackled in from the two-way radio. "But Thom, you know how careful we have to be to keep our magical interaction secret from the mortals.[11] You

---

[11] The Wishworks Factory prides itself in making the wishes it fulfills resemble coincidental or "luck-related" circumstances. Many sweepstakes and lottery winners have no idea that their forgotten wish for a million dollars, possibly made while tossing a coin down a wishing well, has resulted in the wish being fulfilled at a later time. Also, the use of overnight-delivery trucks has helped the Factory enormously with the timely delivery of wishes.

know how we work . . . sweepstakes, lotteries, mysterious packages arriving by mail, never letting our magic ways of fulfilling wishes look too obvious! How will you be able to convince the boy that you're who you say you are?" Snifflewiffle sounded concerned.

Candlewick paused before answering. "Dad, I have no choice. I'm going to take Jeannie and Nora in with me. He'll have to believe me when he sees them."

When Snifflewiffle replied, he sounded weary and defeated. "Okay, son, if you must you must. But *please*"— Jeannie and Nora hardly dared to breathe as they listened to Snifflewiffle's instruction—"whatever you do, make sure that the boy understands that he can't make any more wishes! This has gone too far already."

Candlewick finished his call and turned to address the two girls in the backseat.

"Okay, we have clearance." He looked determined. "We're going to tell him the whole truth."

Nora was shocked. "But we'll be in disguise, right?" The tiny leprechaun snapped her fingers and transformed herself back into the makeup lady with glasses. Candlewick shook his head.

"No. No disguises. If he sees you as you really are, I will have a better chance of making him believe me."

Jeannie grimaced. "But my people haven't had direct contact with humans for years." Her eyes hardened. "They were our masters and we were their slaves. I'm sorry, but I can't do it." She crossed her arms defiantly.

Candlewick raised his hand in a placating gesture. "Jeannie, I realize that you have many reasons to mistrust the mortals. But we are talking about a much bigger picture here." He looked at her with sympathy. "If you will do this, I will give you my word." He put his hand on her shoulder. "As the new president, one of the first things I will do is resolve the contract negotiations with your people. You have my promise."

Jeannie said nothing for a moment, then gave Candlewick a piercing look. "I will hold you to that, Mr. Candlewick."[12]

Candlewick smiled. "Okay." He sighed and looked at the magical creatures with resolve. "Let's do this."

---

[12] One should be very careful when making a promise to a Jinn, for they will not forget what you have said and will hold you to your word by a magical bond. There are very few instances of people who have ever broken a promise to a Jinn and not suffered unimaginable torments.

CHAPTER THIRTEEN

The Meeting

Wheeeerooooowr, plink, plunk, braaaaaaaaaap. The horrible sounds that emanated from the beautiful electric guitar sounded like a tortured animal. Benjamin grimaced and consulted his *How to Learn Guitar in Ten Hard Steps* book. After a couple of minutes of study, he laughed and shook his head, wondering why he had bothered with the manual in the first place.

He focused his eyes upon his outstretched fingers in silent concentration. A smile crept across his face as he picked up the guitar once more. In moments, the sunken living room in his spacious bungalow was filled with the melodic strains of a heavy metal ballad.

A loud knock on his door stopped him mid-chorus. Putting down the awesome V-shaped guitar, he moved past the rows of arcade games to the entryway.

"Hello, you're Ben, right?" The man in the blue derby flashed a smile. Ben blinked and scratched his cheek.

"If you're here about the high-speed Internet connection, a guy came out earlier and already installed it."

The man looked bewildered for a moment, then continued.

"Err, no, that isn't what I'm here for. I just wondered if I could talk to you for a minute. It's very important. My name is Thomas Candlewick, and these are my friends . . ."

In spite of all of the amazing things Ben had seen since he made his birthday wish, he was unprepared for the sight of the two creatures standing uncomfortably behind the man, peering around his long legs. Ben boggled at the unearthly beings, hardly able to believe his eyes.

"What are *they*?" Ben asked, awestruck. Jeannie returned Ben's unabashed stare with a look of apprehension and dislike, her trail of smoke turning from its usual healthy pink to a deep crimson.

"Allow me to introduce Jeannie and Nora," Candlewick

replied. "Jeannie is a Jinn, and Nora is a leprechaun."

Ben's eyes nearly popped out of his head. Wow. Maybe he should wish for a Jinn of his own. That would be so cool! But, upon sensing the intense dislike from Jeannie, he decided that perhaps it wouldn't be such a great idea.

Candlewick cleared his throat impatiently. "May we come in?"

After considering this for a moment, Ben nodded, too stunned to speak, and opened the door wider. The visitors entered and looked around appreciatively.

Nora spoke. "I like what you've done with the place."

Ben stared at the tiny girl in the green suit. He managed to mumble, "Thanks."

The man in the derby looked around for someplace to sit. When Ben had wished the elaborate cottage into existence, he had forgotten that he might have visitors.

"Oh! Sorry about that. Just give me a second." Ben, coming to his senses, concentrated on a spot on the floor near Candlewick's feet. Before he could wish for a chair, though, Candlewick interrupted him, waving his hand with some urgency.

"No, don't! It's all right. I'm perfectly comfortable on the floor." He quickly folded his legs under him and sat down on the white shag carpeting.

He knows, Ben thought to himself.

The visitors had to be there because of his birthday wish, but he couldn't figure out why. He decided that the direct approach would be best.

"So, I take it you're here because of my birthday wish?"

Candlewick removed his hat and smiled. "That is precisely the reason that I am here." He removed a glittering pocket watch from his vest and checked the time.

"I work in the wish-fulfillment business." He wound the watch with a small twist of his thumb and index finger. "And I really have to congratulate you. You came up with a doozy!"

Candlewick absently put the watch back in his gray-and-green-striped vest pocket. Ben smiled back broadly, proud of his accomplishment.

"Yeah, well, I really had no idea that it would actually *work*. I mean"—he shrugged—"people make birthday wishes all the time, don't they? How come mine came true?"

Candlewick paused, deciding whether he should answer Ben's question. After a moment he spoke, looking resigned. "The reason it worked is because you followed all of the rules to a T."

He proceeded to reiterate the wishing rules that he explained to every new intern at the Wishworks Factory tour. Ben was impressed with the explanation, and felt much like a person feels when a magician explains the simplicity behind what looks like an impossible magic trick.

Ben whistled softly through his teeth at the implications of this newfound knowledge. "Wow, wait until my friends hear about this . . ."

Jeannie and Nora watched their boss's face flicker with panic and then recover smoothly.

"Well, that would present a problem, and that is also why I am here." He sighed. "Your wish has created a crisis that is bigger than you realize. There is a reason why every person is supposed to make only one wish on his or her birthday."

Ben listened with amazement as Candlewick described the incredible Wishworks Factory and the process involved in making wishes come true. If it weren't for the fantastical creatures that stood before him, he wouldn't have believed it.

Candlewick paced around the spacious living room, wrapping up his explanation with as much persuasive flair as he could manage. "So you see, wishes were created to benefit mankind. They are the living embodiment of all our hopes and dreams. If one person's wish were to steal away the wishes of other children everywhere . . ." He raised his hands in a helpless gesture. ". . . then people would never have anything to believe in, never have the actual experience of seeing a dream come true. The Factory wasn't designed to fulfill the wishes and needs of just one person." His face grew grave and intense. "Without hope, life has no meaning at all."

Ben stayed silent throughout Candlewick's impassioned speech. Only when Candlewick had finished, hoarse and exhausted, did he finally respond.

"Your story really is amazing, and if it wasn't for the fact that I had experienced this whole wish thing for myself, I would have never thought it possible." He glanced at the curling smoke that occupied Jeannie's lower half and shook his head wonderingly.

But then he looked uncomfortable as he gazed helplessly into Candlewick's eyes.

"Here's the thing . . ." He fiddled nervously with the small remote that adjusted the massage settings on his chair. "I . . . I don't want to hurt anybody. I'm really sorry . . ."

Candlewick could see that the boy was in deep conflict. "Can't you see that by creating this wish you could put millions of people out of work? Not to mention what would happen if nobody's wishes came true anymore . . ."

Ben's eyes shone with guilt and he gazed at the floor. Taking away everyone in the world's wishes seemed so selfish!

A new thought struck him. What if he were to make a wish that everyone's wishes everywhere would come true?

He knew it wouldn't work. It would upset the balance of what was natural. He could imagine a world where nobody did anything but wish for what they wanted. If everyone had unlimited wishes, it would destroy the Factory.

He wrestled back and forth, searching for some solution other than to unwish his wish. But in the end, the very thought of going back to his old life at the orphanage and having to endure Mr. Roach making him scrub the horrible slime-filled stew pots, the smell of the moldy dormitory room, and his tiny uncomfortable army cot was too much for him to handle.

"I'm really sorry." Ben wore a pained expression. "I just can't do it."

Candlewick looked disappointed.

Ben's voice took on a pleading tone.

"Try to understand. You don't know what it's like to lose your parents and to be alone." Ben's face crumbled. "To have your parents with you one day and gone the next." Ben stared out the window at the orphanage. "And then to end up with horrible people who hate you." He turned back to Candlewick with a sorrowful expression on his face. "Wouldn't you do anything to change your life if you could?"

To Ben's surprise, Candlewick seemed at a loss for words.

"As a matter of fact, I do know what that feels like." Candlewick sighed, picked up his hat, and walked stiffly to the door. Then, with his hand on the doorknob, he said thoughtfully, "But I didn't steal other people's dreams to make my own come true."

Ben stared after the trio and felt a renewed surge of guilt and shame. He gathered Rags, who had been sleeping in a patch of sunlight by the window, into his arms and stroked the terrier's curly coat.

He had no idea what he should do.

CHAPTER FOURTEEN

Disaster Strikes!

"*I* can't believe it, Thom, I just can't!" Perkins said, mopping his brow with a large polka-dotted handkerchief.

Candlewick paced nervously in his cluttered office, hoping beyond hope that what Perkins had just told him hadn't really happened.

"Have you searched everywhere?" Candlewick asked his quivering assistant. "I mean *everywhere*. Did you try the Shamrock field?"

"Yes."

"How about the boardroom?"

"Yes, I checked it."

"Underneath the Globe Maker itself?"

Perkins shrugged, looking helpless. "I'm telling you, I looked! I even checked the Funicula to see if the security team dropped it on the way to the vault."

Candlewick ran a trembling hand through his hair. He hadn't expected to return to Wishworks and find that the Unlimited Wish Globe had vanished. It seemed impossible! Everyone in the Factory knew what was at stake. Unless . . .

"Perk. Who did you last see with the globe? Was it my dad?"

Perkins thought for a moment and nodded. "Yeah. After you rushed off, he had the globe." He shifted his feet uncomfortably. "It was just Simon and me in the room with him. I asked if there was anything I could do, and when Snifflewiffle said no, I left to help sort out the mess on the Factory floor."

Candlewick gazed out the plate-glass window at the whirring machinery, lost in thought. Only high-ranking company officers knew how to unlock the Wish Globes.

The only person Candlewick could think of that would be capable of using a Wish Globe for his own diabolical purposes was Thornblood, the ruler of the Curseworks Factory.

Candlewick's eyes hardened with sudden realization.

"I knew that my brother was being way too nice in there," he murmured. Smacking his fist into his palm, he said, "Call the guys over at the Thaumaturgic Cardioscope. Tell them to focus the scope on Simon Spinchley. I need to know exactly where he is." Candlewick hesitated, his mind racing. "And send for Warren, Wallace, and Wimbledon. We're going to need them, as well."

Perkins looked surprised. "I don't understand."

Candlewick's eyes hardened. "Simon is a traitor, Perk. He's working for Thornblood." Perkins's jaw sagged and his face turned pale.

"But . . ."

Candlewick grabbed his hat and marched to the door, his face set and determined.

"Where are you going?" Perkins called after him.

"To get the kid and set this whole thing straight before it's too late!"

≈ CHAPTER FIFTEEN ≈

A New Wish

After Candlewick left Ben's luxurious sunken living room, Ben gazed at his guitar, his newly acquired video game collection, and his indoor basketball hoop, and scowled.

It just wasn't fair. He had endured so many hard months living at the orphanage and felt that he was finally getting something in return. Didn't he deserve a break?

Yes, but whose wishes did you steal to get all of this stuff?

Ben's conscience prickled uncomfortably. He glanced over at the picture of his parents at the beach, the one that he had kept so carefully among his meager treasures, a picture that was now expensively framed and sitting on a shelf above the elegant brick fireplace.

He had a sudden memory of how involved his mother had been with charity organizations; how she had devoted her life to helping people who were less fortunate than her own family. When Ben was little he used to feel uncomfortable going with his mom as she made her rounds to the homeless shelters in downtown Los Angeles, handing out clothing and sandwiches to the grateful recipients.

He knew then that his mom wouldn't approve of what he was doing. Neither would his dad, for that matter. They had been the most caring people that Ben had ever known, his entire world.

Just one more wish, that's all. Then I'll stop.

His heart soared with new inspiration. Why hadn't he thought of it before? It was in front of him the whole time and he hadn't seen it. There was a wish that he hadn't made, a secret, burning desire that he hardly dared entertain when it entered his mind. It was unthinkable. It was impossible. And yet he couldn't deny that it was the wish that was nearest and dearest to his soul.

Motes of dust flickered like glowing embers as the fading afternoon sunlight streamed through his new home's elegant stained-glass windows. Ben sat cross-legged on the floor, cradling the framed photograph of his parents on his lap.

Memories of the day of the plane crash rushed into his head. He had been spending the week at his friend Adam Messerschmidt's house while his parents attended a conference in England. He and Adam were deep in the middle of a game of Super Mario Kart when Mrs. Messerschmidt entered the room, her normally cheerful face looking drawn and haggard. She motioned for Ben to follow her to the kitchen, where she told him the terrible news. As she said the words, Ben felt like he was a million miles away, like he was looking at her through the wrong end of a telescope. His parents had told him that they would only be away for a week, but it had turned into a lifetime.

He closed his eyes and concentrated, thinking of their faces. It was time to turn back the clock; to go back to that fateful day and change the very thing that had turned his life from a happy dream into a nightmare worse than he could have ever imagined. He tried to ignore the nagging thought that such a wish shouldn't be made. Something wasn't right about it, but he couldn't help himself.

I wish that my parents were back—that they would be at the door right now, ready to take me home.

Ben waited a moment, hardly daring to breathe. He

cracked one eye open, then, seeing nothing, strode to the window and looked out at the empty driveway, waiting for the sounds of a car engine.

Any second now. His breath was coming in shallow, quick gasps. His ears strained for the sound he most wanted to hear.

THUMP! THUMP! THUMP! The loud pounding on his front door startled him. Trembling with anticipation, he walked to the door. *Did it work?* Tears burned in his eyes. They could be right there on the other side of the door waiting for him. He could almost see his mom and dad's smiling faces, almost feel their arms wrap around him like he had envisioned them doing countless times when he had cried himself to sleep in the orphanage.

With a shaky hand, he pulled open the heavy door.

≈ Chapter Sixteen ≈

Curseworks

"**S**o, you've come."

The light of the green fire that illuminated the pocked and twisted chamber cast a sickly pallor over the elegant form of Adolfus Thornblood, the CEO of Curseworks. Simon looked nervously at the floor, unable to make contact with the glowing eyes of the lavishly dressed president, who wore an impeccable black suit and silken top hat.

"Y-y-yes, master." His words sounded frail and faltering, far less assured than he had hoped. The gaunt president's mouth twitched as he motioned to the shadowy mass of twisted beasts lurking in the corner.

There were hissing giggles, then the sound of hundreds of insect legs clicking as the misshapen forms scuttled across the stone floor. Simon felt the bile rise in his throat and tried not to retch when the stench of the creatures reached his nostrils. These were the cursed employees, nicknamed Thornblood's Spider Monkeys by the Wishworks personnel. They were the twisted forms of those who chose to leave Wishworks and turn their lives over to Thornblood's service.[13]

The rumors that these creatures had once been human, Jinn, or fair folk traveled throughout the Wishing Lands. Simon hadn't believed that they were true until now.

But I'm different, he reassured himself. *I'm Leo Snifflewiffle's son and Thornblood wouldn't dare turn me into one of the vile creatures. After all, I was in line to be president of the Factory!*

Disfigured apelike faces grinned up at him, baring broken, yellow teeth. The front halves of their black, hairy bodies resembled monkeys, but then, like a creature from a

---

[13] The exact number of employees that have quit Wishworks and gone to Curseworks is not known, but what *is* known are the most popular answers given by employees as to their reasons "why" during exit interviews conducted at the Wishworks Human Resources department. "Thornblood is offering me more money and job security" is the most popular reason, followed by "I want to be tortured by an evil overlord, enjoy terrible working conditions, and try living as a foul-smelling monster with spider's legs for the rest of my life" as the distant second.

living nightmare, their bottom halves extended horribly into the bulbous abdomens of spiders.

Simon's hand shook as he took the small bag of coins offered by the nearest creature and shivered as he felt his hand brush the leathery, ice-cold skin.

"This isn't what we agreed!" Simon examined the contents of the opened pouch with indignation. He forced himself to meet Thornblood's stare and mustered the courage to continue. "Y-you said I would be taken care of, that I would have job security and a pay raise. This is practically nothing!"

Thornblood gave a sinister chuckle. "You are correct. I did say that you would be taken care of, and I never break a promise." He nodded to the nearest of the cursed creatures, who grinned and began to advance on Simon.

"W-what about Thomas Candlewick? You promised me my revenge!"

The apelike hands closed around Simon's wrists and arms. Thornblood smiled coldly. "Oh, don't worry about that. I assure you, I have my own reasons for wanting Candlewick to suffer."

Simon's voice rose to a high-pitched scream. "Wait, I can give you the names of everyone who works at the Factory! We can make a deal!" The surging tide of Spider Monkeys lifted his struggling body into the air. "You can't do this to me, I'm an executive!"

Thornblood motioned for the creatures to take the prisoner away. More creatures flooded into the hall and joined their companions, hissing with delight as they hoisted the screaming Simon into the air and carried him through the dank corridor.

Thornblood watched the swarming creatures leave the room. He reached into the pocket of his expensive coat and, removing the globe, gazed at Ben's unlimited wishes. Thornblood smiled. It had been a long time of watching and waiting, but finally the day had come. The power source for his wonderfully diabolical machine, the machine that would transform the weakest curse into a living, dragonish monster, was nearly complete. And it had been purchased at such an easy price.

After locking the globe inside a heavily bolted vault, Thornblood walked down a long stairway leading to the chamber that held his invention. Leaning on an iron balcony overlooking the floor, he felt a surge of pride.

Red light emanated from the contraption's inner depths. Steam hissed from cracks in its blackened iron surface, and swarming Spider Monkeys attended to the final stages of the machine's completion.

His beautiful invention, which he had aptly named the Curse-atina, possessed large pipes that extended out the top, but were cut short as if waiting for another set of fittings to join to them. Beneath the pipes was an expansive, wicked-looking organ whose pale keys were made from human bones.

Thornblood studied the progress and drummed his fingers on the railing. He was anxious to have the instrument completed, and his fingers itched to tickle the hideous keys.

With the Unlimited Wish Globe now in his possession, he was able to achieve the impossible. His Curse-atina would do something that his old machinery never could: generate so many dragonlike curses at once, each more powerful than the one before, that *every* single wish created to stop them would be destroyed. No longer would curses be so easily defeated by the slightest good intention from a well-wisher.[14]

His thin lips curved upward in a cruel smile, and he adjusted the brim of his silken hat.

Thornblood contemplated his battle strategy. He would

---

[14] The term "well-wisher" originated, not surprisingly, from a label given to people predisposed to casting coins in wishing wells. This simple and casual wish should not be underestimated, however, for they have been very effective in thwarting countless potential curses over the centuries.

start by destroying Wishworks, eliminating any chance of the Factory interfering with his plans. The Spider Monkeys would lead the attack. Then he would follow the first wave of Spider Monkeys with a horde of his deadly curses.

He laughed silently. Wishworks would never withstand such an onslaught! And following the demise of his oldest enemy, he would release his new and improved curses upon all of humanity.

His eyes glinted.

He had waited very patiently for his day of triumph, and now it was just around the corner.

"Master, the newest recruit is ready for inspection." The wrinkled face of his oldest and ugliest worker grinned up at him.

Thornblood nodded and followed his hobbling servant from the chamber, swinging his tapered walking stick.

He emerged a few moments later inside of a room that was almost as large as the one that held the Curse-atina.

It looked like a torture chamber from a medieval dungeon. Endless tables with iron hooks and leather straps lined one wall. On another, vials of viscous liquids in dirty glass beakers were crowded on splintered tabletops. The table nearest to Thornblood held a pile of neatly folded clothes—the clothes that Simon Spinchley Snifflewiffle had been wearing minutes before.

A shrill whistle screeched, followed by the sounds of hundreds of scuttling feet. Twisted Spider Monkeys poured from web-strewn cracks and crevices high above the chamber floor, some spilling to the ground like insects swept from a tabletop, others spinning themselves downward like spiders. Soon they were all assembled, grinning their broken smiles, their small, tangled chests heaving.

Thornblood stood in front of his henchmen, his delicate, gloved hands clasped behind his back. His gaze rested on the quivering creatures, who tried their best to look fearless and at attention.

At the end of the first row, the newest servant quaked with fear, unaccustomed to the hideous form it now possessed. Thornblood approached the new recruit and took its simian face roughly in his hands. He rocked its head from side to side in grim inspection. The creature's lips curled back, exposing two neat rows of exceptionally white teeth.

"So, Simon, how do you like your new body?"

Simon whimpered.

"I w-w-want to be me again." He groveled at Thornblood's shiny black shoes. "Please, change me back. Please . . ."

Thornblood laughed lightly and knelt, then grasped Simon hard by the nape of the neck. Simon let out a yelp.

Thornblood drew himself up to full height, raising the creature's eyes to his own. The spidery legs struggled helplessly.

"You work for me now, Simon." His words came out with a hiss. "And at Curseworks you have the *ultimate* job security. For once you are hired . . ." He dropped the shaking Spider Monkey with a sickening thud. ". . . you never leave." The other Spider Monkeys screeched and howled with laughter. Thornblood motioned for two guards to take Simon.

Thornblood strode from the room and the Spider Monkeys crept back into the shadows. They didn't see the other forms emerge from behind a torture machine— the metal men that had carefully hidden themselves and witnessed the terrible exchange.

Their electric eyes glowed steadily in the dark as they exchanged meaningful glances. This was why they had been sent. Brass keys spinning and clicking quietly in their well-formed brass heads, the trio exited through a window and were gone without a sound.

CHAPTER SEVENTEEN

A Turn of Events

*B*en was totally unprepared for what he saw as he opened his front door—not his parents, but the red and fuming faces of Ms. Pinch and Mr. Roach.

"So, you think you can get away with making us your personal slaves, do you?" Mr. Roach's eyes bulged from their sockets, and Ben noticed a large purple vein pulsing madly on his shiny forehead.

Ben, acting quickly, tried to muster up another wish. *I wish that they would do anything I say.*

Nothing happened.

Ben panicked. "Wait, I . . . I can explain."

But before he had the chance, Mr. Roach took his arm in a viselike grip, dragged him from his living room, and threw him outside. Ben was sent sprawling painfully to the gravel path.

"You're gonna get it now," Mr. Roach growled at Ben. "When I get through with you, you'll wish you could go back to scrubbing my stew pots."

Ben's stomach turned. What had happened? With growing panic, he realized that his wishes weren't working anymore! He tried several times to wish for anything, that the two adults would be turned into harmless white mice, or shoes, or even babies, but nothing worked!

Mr. Roach approached slowly, a tiger about to sink its claws into its helpless prey. "You. I'll teach you a thing or two. Make a fool out of Solomon Roach, will ya?"

Ben tried to make a dash for his front door but was apprehended by the lightning-fast grip of Ms. Pinch. The woman's sharp, yellow nails dug deep into his flesh, making him cry out with agony.

Suddenly there was a crack of thunder and a burst of golden light. Ms. Pinch lost her grip on Ben, and a figure with two powerful arms grabbed him and hoisted him over his shoulder.

Mr. Roach, momentarily stunned, recovered and ran over. "STOP!" Howling like an enraged animal, he dove for the silhouetted man. He landed just short of the man's ankle. The golden light flared with white-hot intensity. The burst of light was followed by an earth-shattering *KABOOM!*

When the smoke and dust cleared, Benjamin Bartholomew Piff was gone.

⊰ Chapter Eighteen ⊱

Ben's Mission

*C*andlewick gazed down at Ben who lay unconscious on the couch in Snifflewiffle's office. This was the usual reaction when somebody from earth jolted into the dimension where Wishworks existed.

Candlewick stirred his hot cup of coffee mechanically, a small frown on his face as he thought of the danger that Ben had narrowly escaped. Nothing upset him more than seeing a child victimized by an adult. He went to his father's desk and pushed a switch. A small, sleek laptop computer slid out from a hidden compartment. He typed in *Benjamin*

Bartholomew Piff. Ben's file popped up on the screen and Candlewick scanned the information. A pained look crossed his face when he scrolled down to a tiny newspaper clipping about the tragic plane crash that took Ben's parents' lives.

He clicked on a folder titled *Birthday Wishes* and opened it up. A small box appeared, which listed each birthday Ben had had since his first. Next to each number, one through ten, was a place to list comments. None of Ben's previous birthday wishes had ever come true.

Poor kid, Candlewick mused as he clicked the small X to close the window. *He finally gets a chance at happiness, is clever enough to pull it off, and ends up making a wish that could potentially destroy all the happiness in the world.*

There was stirring on the couch as Ben groggily lifted his head. He gazed around the office of former president Snifflewiffle in awe. High vaulted ceilings with soaring beams, each carved with magical gnome and fairy figures, extended to the ceiling. At the apex was a circular stained-glass window, and colorful beams of light cast patterns on the ornate walls. Next to Ben was a gigantic brass elephant covered with interesting knobs and switches.

"If you're thirsty, just press that button on the side of his trunk." Candlewick smiled at Ben. Ben rose from the couch and inspected the brass creature. Reaching out, he pushed the red button on the elephant's long nose. The gears whirred and clicked to life, and from someplace deep inside, the mechanical beast made a very lifelike trumpeting sound. A small goblet was lowered from the trunk, and a nozzle filled the cup with a sparkling purple liquid.[15]

Ben had never tasted anything so good. It was better than the best soda pop he had ever had. Smiling at Candlewick, he nodded his approval. Then a thoughtful expression crossed his face.

"So this is the world where all wishes come from?" Ben asked. It was difficult to comprehend.

Candlewick pulled up a comfortable-looking wingback chair and sat, smiling kindly. "Yes, and I apologize for bringing you up here without your consent. But, unfortunately, the

---

[15] The brass elephant has been a staple at the Factory since 1952. The drink that it dispenses is extracted from a rare berry that was accidentally discovered by Leo Snifflewiffle when he was a small boy on a family vacation in the Swiss Alps. Young Leo had been sledding down the Matterhorn and would have flown right off of the side of a mountainous cliff if it hadn't been for a helpful St. Bernard that grabbed the seat of his pants and saved him. The large dog carried a barrelful of the liquid around its neck, and after Leo sampled some of the delicious drink, he was led to a secret Alpine village that grew the berries used to make the special formula. The drink has the very special side effect of causing anyone who imbibes to grow an additional toe in their old age, and many retired Wishworks employees swear that the extra appendage is both a useful improvement and a wonderful conversation piece.

circumstances forced me to do it. You understand?" He looked meaningfully at Ben.

"I think you came at the right time. I'm not complaining." Ben shuddered, remembering Mr. Roach and Ms. Pinch.

"You know," Ben continued, "I was only going to make one more wish. Then I would have stopped, I promise."

Candlewick read Ben's thoughts. His face grew compassionate.

"Look, Ben, I know that life has been pretty hard for you down there. And if it was in my power to allow you to keep your wish, I would."

Ben said nothing but stared down at the ground. It had been so nice to have the chance to make his dreams come true.

Hesitating, he asked Candlewick the question that was now burning inside him.

"Is the reason that my wishes stopped coming true because I was mean to Ms. Pinch and Mr. Roach?" Ben glanced up at Candlewick guiltily.

Candlewick chuckled. "No, it's actually more complicated than that. But I will say"—Candlewick's eyes twinkled—"it's a good thing you didn't let your, ah, *punishment* of them go any further than you did. You might have started edging into curse territory."

A door at the far side of the room opened and the diminutive Leo Snifflewiffle emerged. He carried a silver tray of his favorite cookies, and, smiling widely, set them down in front of Ben.

"Welcome to Wishworks, young man," he said.

Ben looked up at Candlewick questioningly.

"Ben, this is my father, Leo Snifflewiffle, the president of Wishworks," Candlewick explained. Ben shook the small hand the man offered.

Leo wagged his finger at Candlewick. "Ex-president. Thom here is the new president. Newly elected," he clarified. He turned a sympathetic look at Candlewick. "I only wish that you had inherited the position in easier times, son."

Candlewick nodded and his face grew grave. "Did Wallace, Warren, and Wimbledon make it back yet?"

Leo nodded. "Yes, a couple of minutes ago. I have ordered them sent up here to meet us at once." Leo moved over to an old-fashioned-looking telephone, lifted the black earpiece, and spoke.

"Send in the spies, please."

Moments later the doors opened and in walked three brass robots. The first was tall and lanky, wore a derby and a monocle, and had a drooping silver mustache. The second was short and squat with wheels for feet and had a metallic

Napoleonic hat perched on his round head. The last had strange clawlike feet and carried a set of brass bagpipes. Fascinated, Ben watched the clockwork keys rotate in the robots' heads, processing their thoughts.[16]

"Gentlemen. Your report, please?" Snifflewiffle pronounced his words carefully. The machines required very precise enunciation to process a request. There was a brief whirring and clicking, then the first robot, Wimbledon, conveyed his report with a rattling English accent.

"Sir. The globule that contained the wish made by Benjamin Bartholomew Piff was placed into a vault by Thornblood, commander of the Curseworks Factory, at precisely 1800 hours on July the seventh. It was delivered by Simon Spinchley, who was taken into captivity shortly after."

Candlewick leaned down confidentially to Ben. "That is the reason your wishes stopped working."

Wallace, the bagpiper, clumped forward and snapped

---

[16] Warren, Wallace, and Wimbledon were created to be the secret eyes and ears of Wishworks in 1904 by then-president Penelope Thicklepick. It is said that the incredible clockwork robots were designed by Thomas Edison on a secret commission from the Factory, and that while designing the robots in his basement in Menlo Park, he perfected his motion-picture process and released his first silent film shortly after. The robots have proven to be invaluable to the Factory and need very little maintenance, being powered by some of the most intricate gear mechanisms ever designed.

a salute to Candlewick. "Sir. It has come to our attention that Thornblood has plans to launch an invasion, with the intention to overthrow the Wishworks Factory by utilizing a secret weapon of his own design."

Ben watched, mesmerized, as Wimbledon pressed a button on the back of Warren, the stocky robot. A small movie projector emerged from the robot's metal hat and aimed itself at a wall. A grainy, black-and-white image of Thornblood's Curse-atina appeared.

Wallace continued in his Scottish burr. "Once implemented, the device will convert the Unlimited Wish Globe's power into an inexhaustible source of energy for the machine, thereby enhancing the power of curses by 352.4 percent and effectively eliminating the counteractive properties of any well-meaning wish." The projector shut off as the brass man finished his report, his metal jaw going slack, and the three robots resumed their attentive stances.

A heavy silence fell upon the room.

Snifflewiffle cleared his throat and thanked the robots, who saluted in turn and left the office.

"It seems to be getting worse and worse." Snifflewiffle removed his glasses and rubbed the lenses with a handkerchief. "I should never have trusted Simon. I didn't expect . . ." His voice trailed off.

Candlewick walked over and laid a comforting hand on his father's shoulder.

"It's okay, Dad. We'll figure out what to do." He looked over at Ben, who shifted his feet in discomfort.

"Ben," Candlewick began. "Thornblood's machine could destroy not only Wishworks, but also everyone on earth. Every evil thing anybody wishes could come true. Curses are bad things, horrible ways to torture people." He walked over to Ben and kneeled down next to him so that he could look into his eyes.

"How many kids do you know that have, in a fit of anger, wished for something terrible to happen to somebody that they weren't getting along with? If Thornblood finishes his machine . . ." He trailed off.

Ben's mind reeled at the impact of what Candlewick was saying. He himself had, at times, wished that Mr. Roach would crumple up and die, or that Ms. Pinch would never have been born. It was one thing to think those things, but he wouldn't want to be responsible if they ever came true.

Candlewick sighed. "I know it's all pretty hard to believe, but you are the only person that can stop it all from happening. You have to unwish your wish."

Ben nodded mutely. As badly as he wanted his own life to change, he was a good-hearted boy, and he realized now that his own needs couldn't meet the cost of destroying everyone else's chances for happiness.

"Okay. I'll do it," Ben said solemnly. "So I just wish for it to be undone right now, and everything will go back to normal?"

Candlewick shook his head. "Now that the wish is imprisoned in the Curseworks vault, you must first recapture the Wish Globe. Once you're in possession of the globe, you must get outside of the Curseworks walls before you can unwish the wish. Thornblood made sure that his Factory was completely wish-proof." Candlewick shrugged sympathetically. "I'm sorry. It really is the only way."

Ben nodded, too overcome to speak.

Candlewick turned back to his father. "We don't have much time, Dad. If Thornblood is putting together his army, then it must mean that his machine is almost finished. We'd better let everyone know that we need to prepare for a fight."

Candlewick motioned for Ben to follow. As the two exited the office, Candlewick spoke.

"Tomorrow morning we'll start training you for the mission. You'll have to learn how to defend yourself."

Ben's heart thumped in his chest. *Fight?* He hadn't thought of that.

"Don't worry, you'll be trained by the best." Candlewick tousled Ben's hair. "Now, let's get you to your quarters. There's a great little place right by the Cardioscope that I think you'll like."

Ben followed Candlewick through the sprawling city to a small cottage. Inside the cozy house was a small bed and other furnishings, including a table laden with a tray of small cakes and a pot of hot tea. Ben noticed with a surge of gratitude that the bed was covered with fresh linen, the sheets folded back in a welcoming way.

"Make yourself at home." Candlewick indicated a phone that matched the one Ben had seen in Snifflewiffle's office. "Oh, and if you need anything at all, just call. I'll be by tomorrow at nine o'clock sharp to take you on a quick tour of Wishworks before we get you started at the training grounds."

Candlewick patted Ben on the shoulder and moved toward the door. Ben hesitated a moment and then called after him. "Mr. Candlewick?"

Candlewick stopped mid-stride and turned back to the boy. Ben, looking uncomfortable, shifted his feet.

"I . . . forgot to say thank you for saving me earlier."

Candlewick stared at Ben for a full five seconds. Those were the words he had never heard in all his years as a

Wishmaker, the words that he thought children everywhere had completely forgotten. Stunned but happy, he gave the boy a small tip of his hat and replied.

"You're welcome, Ben."

≈ CHAPTER NINETEEN ≈
Battlerang Training

Thump thump thump! "Ben? It's Thom. Are you ready to go?"

Ben woke with a start. Suddenly he remembered where he was and what had happened the night before.

"Be there in a sec!"

He threw on his jeans and sweatshirt and opened the front door. Candlewick smirked at his tousled bed-hair and pointed to the hands on his ornate pocket watch. "Nine o'clock sharp, remember?"

Ben grinned sheepishly. His bed was so soft and

comfortable that he had inadvertently overslept. After brushing his teeth and throwing on a pair of sneakers, Ben joined Candlewick outside. They chatted animatedly as they strode down the winding stone path to their first destination, the Feathered Funicula.

Now, if there was one thing that filled Ben with paralyzing fear, it was flying. Ever since his parents' plane crash, Ben had sworn to keep his feet planted firmly on the ground. Consequently, when he came in sight of the flying chairs, Ben's stomach lurched.

"No way. I'm sorry, Mr. Candlewick, but there is no way I can go up in one of those *things*." Ben studied the slowly revolving chairs with apprehension.

"Oh, come on, you'll love it." Candlewick's eyes sparkled with enthusiasm. "Once you're up there, it's just like floating on a cloud. There's nothing like it in the whole world."

Before Ben could protest further, Candlewick threw the switch. Two chairs winged their way down, settling gently in front of them. Ben gulped.

"Are you sure they're safe?" He inspected a chair's large striped cushion. "I don't see any seat belts."

"That's because once your feet rest on the footstool like this . . ." Candlewick hopped into one of the seats and demonstrated. ". . . you're firmly locked in. It's better than a seat belt; there's no way you can fall out. Try it."

Ben reluctantly sat as Candlewick instructed. As soon as his feet touched the footstool, he felt an invisible force hold him in as if two unseen hands were pressing on his chest. *This isn't so bad,* he thought. *Maybe it only hovers a foot or two off the ground.*

But before Ben could prepare himself with a countdown of some kind, Candlewick pressed a button and with a loud *whoosh,* the two chairs leaped into the skies.

"Look down on your left! There's the Thaumaturgic Cardioscope!" Candlewick's excited voice crackled over the speaker near Ben's right ear. Ben hazarded a glance downward, then squeezed his eyes shut in alarm. They were so high up!

The chairs swooped over the dazzling minarets of the Fulfillment department of the Factory. "See," Candlewick's voice crackled. "This isn't so bad, huh?"

"Yeah, it's . . . really great." Ben's voice came in short gasps, and he kept his eyes tightly shut. Candlewick chatted on about the view, unaware that his reluctant passenger was missing it all.

Only when the chairs swept into the tunnel leading to the Fulfillment department did Ben open his eyes. He was greeted by the sight of the long, winding, colorful tubes that processed all the Factory's wishes.

Candlewick steered the chairs up to the workstation where Delores, looking harried, busily sorted Wish Cards.

"Hi, Dee. I have somebody that I'd like you to meet." Candlewick smiled and indicated Ben. "This is Benjamin Piff."

"Okay, Thom, I'll be right with . . ." The pretty brunette paused mid-count. "You're Benjamin Bartholomew Piff?"

Ben nodded. Delores raised her eyebrows and pursed her lips before replying coolly, "I assume you have no idea what trouble that wish of yours has caused us. I have been up to my ears in canceled wishes, and I've got heartbroken kids all over the place! Not to mention the paperwork! I'm drowning in Wish Cards—"

Candlewick interrupted the woman's rant. "He knows, Dee. And he's sorry." He put his hand on Ben's shoulder. "We're going to fix everything, right, Ben?" Ben nodded, embarrassed.

Delores's expression softened. "Well, I suppose you couldn't have known," she said.

"We have to keep moving," Candlewick said. "I need to get Ben over to the Battlerang training grounds." He smiled reassuringly at Delores as their chairs floated away. "Don't worry, we'll get this whole thing sorted out."

The chairs landed next to a big field with a horseshoe-shaped building, and a portly man jogged up to meet them. Candlewick helped Ben out of his chair and introduced him. "Ben, this is my assistant, Perkins."

Ben shook the bespectacled man's outstretched hand. Perkins smiled warmly. "Pleased to meet you, Ben. Glad you decided to join us."

Ben followed the two men through a pair of double doors. Most of the lights were off, and Ben was instructed to wait in the foyer until some others arrived. He could just make out several large humpy shapes, black against the shadows. He had barely time to register this when a group of people came over to him.

"So, this is the guy that caused all the problems."

Ben's eyes grew round as he gazed up at the scowling Jinn.

"Oh, Gene, give him a break." A thin boy with freckles turned to Ben.

"The name's Pickles. Jonathan Pickles. And this is Gene, Jeannie, Nora, and Fizzle. We just started here as interns three days ago. And I was out sick one day for my allergies. I'm fine now," he said, tapping his nose. "Nasal spray."

Ben recognized the girl Jinn and the leprechaun from their visit at the orphanage. Jeannie regarded him coolly, but the leprechaun offered him a lopsided grin. Ben was speechless.

"Doesn't seem smart enough to make a wish that could destroy the world, does he?" Gene, who obviously had a bad temper, whispered loudly to the fairy. Fizzle shot him a dirty look, and, flapping her gossamer wings, flew up level with Ben's eyes.

"Ignore him, Ben. He's just giving you a hard time because you're *human*." The pretty girl gave him a wink and whispered, "I think you made a very clever wish." She turned to the others. "It's not his fault, you know. He didn't know it was so dangerous."

Suddenly the chamber erupted into spotlights, which revealed the lumpy silhouettes that Ben had seen earlier. Several flying chairs were positioned around the room, outfitted with armor plating, transparent windows covering seats in the front and back, and what looked like small cannons. Jonathan Pickles nudged Ben with his elbow and whispered.

"Man, that is one sick ride, huh?"

Ben nodded as the interns murmured appreciatively. All kinds of interesting weaponry lined the walls of the room. He was about to get a closer look when Candlewick stepped into the beam of a spotlight.

"Good afternoon." He wore a solemn and serious expression. "You will have noticed by now that we are in the process of adapting the Feathered Funicula chairs for battle." Everyone nodded. Candlewick gestured expansively. "This is the Wishworks War Room, and it hasn't been utilized since the time of the Great Wishworks War."[17]

The interns gaped at the massive chamber. Candlewick waited a moment, then continued. "You have been brought here for training on a special mission. Those of you who are interns"—he glanced meaningfully at the others surrounding Ben—"should know that this is a rare opportunity indeed. Should you see the mission to its goal, you will be made into full-fledged Factory employees." Candlewick gave a small, tight-lipped grin. "Instead of the usual ten-year evaluation period." Evidently this was unheard of, because the interns erupted into excited talk. Candlewick motioned for silence.

---

[17] The Great Wishworks War (1904–1917 A.D.) was the worst and bloodiest battle fought in the Factory's history. A group of evil Jinns led by their fearsome commander, the only Jinn known to date who openly used his name, Abul-Cadabra, fought for dominance of the Factory and created the very first curse-enhancing device, the dreaded Lamp of One Thousand Nightmares. The historic annals in the Wishworks Research Library state that this terrible weapon could generate curses of such strength and power that they were almost impossible to stop. Fortunately, due to the ingenuity of Finneas Cheeseweasle, an array of amazing defensive weapons used to combat the Jinns was invented, and the Factory was saved.

"Our spies have revealed that Thornblood has obtained a list of every Wishworks employee from a traitor who will remain unnamed." Most of the workers had already heard about Simon Spinchley's betrayal, but they didn't say anything.

"Fortunately, he doesn't know about *all* of you. Interns are not officially registered in employee rosters, and for that reason we feel confident that you will be able to sneak into his fortress undetected.

"Stealing the Wish Globe from underneath Thornblood's nose will be very dangerous. Should you decide not to accept this mission, you will be welcomed back to the Factory and may continue the job to which you are assigned." He paused for a reaction, but everyone seemed resolute. Ben looked down at Nora and caught a faint look of apprehension on her face, but it changed quickly to something more neutral. Ben stared at the flying chairs and felt his stomach turn. *Will the mission involve going up in one of those things again?*

"Now then. If you will follow me, we will have our first demonstration."

They went to the wall of weaponry where a short woman waited, clad in a blue Wishworks uniform.

"This is Bridgit O'Reilly. She is the Battlechief from the Falling Stars department and will be instructing you in the use of the most ancient of the Wishworks weapons, the Battlerang."

The woman with the close-cropped hair smiled. "Thank you, Thom."

As Candlewick left the room, he shot Ben a quick, reassuring smile. Ben waved and then turned to listen to Ms. O'Reilly as she held up what looked like a small boomerang. "The use of the Wishworks Battlerang originated in the thirteenth century and was brought to us by then-president Wadsworth Pfefferminz."[18] She passed the weapon to Jonathan Pickles, who looked at it and passed it to Ben. Its surface was unadorned except for the delicately inscribed words, *What goes around, comes around.* He smiled at the apt inscription before passing the weapon to Jeannie.

"Some of you may be familiar with the earthly version of this weapon, but I assure you that the Wishworks Battlerang is a different weapon entirely."

When the Battlerang was passed back to Bridgit, she placed a pair of dark-lensed goggles over her eyes and a

---

[18] This was completely accidental. Pfefferminz was trying to invent a heated back-scratcher and, frustrated by the lack of functionality of the device he had created, he attempted to throw it away. To his surprise, the device came spinning back at him, and he only barely managed duck out of the way as it shaved off the lower half of his beard.

leather gauntlet over her right hand. Then she pressed a hidden button on the underside of the Battlerang. The weapon glowed with a white, laserlike intensity. Perkins appeared, holding similar pairs of the protective lenses and gauntlets for the rest of the group to put on.

"Watch carefully." The lithe instructor nodded to Perkins, who threw a switch activating three targets on the far side of the vast chamber. Ben squinted into the distance and could see that the targets were shaped like twisted, monkeylike monsters. Bridgit cocked her arm back and then cast the Battlerang forward in a mighty throw. As it spun at the targets, the weapon emitted a high-pitched scream. There was a blinding flash as the targets were cut through neatly. Ben could smell the targets burning as the Battlerang soared around the other side of the chamber, completing its arc, and landed neatly back in Ms. O'Reilly's hand. The interns whooped and applauded.

Bridgit took off her goggles and smiled.

"It will take some practice, so we'd better get started. Please go to the weapons wall on your left and choose a Battlerang."

Ben was eager to give the Battlerang a try. He wasn't very good at sports, but ever since he laid eyes on the Battlerang, he thought it reminded him of something. Choosing a blue

Battlerang, it came to him. His favorite video game, Outback Hunter, took place in the Australian outback. Would throwing the boomerang-like weapon be anything like the game?

Ben waited patiently while the others took turns throwing at the targets. Most of the Battlerangs careened around the room, wildly out of control, and one narrowly missed hitting Perkins, who ducked just in time behind a flying chair. When it was his turn to throw, Ben was elbowed roughly as the hulking form of Gene shoved him aside.

"Outta my way, mortal."

Gene had the best throw of the interns, but his toss barely nicked the edge of the target, and the weapon flew back well over his reach, crashing with a shower of sparks into a light fixture.

He smirked at Ben as he glided back to the end of the line.

Ben moved hesitantly to take his spot at the throwing area. Ignoring the snort from Gene, Ben cocked his arm back and flung the Battlerang forward as hard as he could.

There was a whistling sound and a giant flash as the weapon spun in a perfect arc and sliced neatly through two of the three targets. Ben's eyes remained riveted on the spinning weapon and he timed his catch perfectly as it returned. The interns gaped in astonishment. Bridgit whipped her goggles off in surprise and turned to Ben.

"Where did you learn to throw like that?" Her voice was incredulous. Ben grinned broadly.

"Outback Hunter."

Bridgit patted his shoulder. "Well, whoever Outback Hunter is, he knows a thing or two about teaching Battlerang drills."

Jonathan Pickles punched him playfully in the arm and, grinning broadly, whispered. "Nice throw, squirt!"

Ben grinned back and said, "Thanks."

"Beginner's luck," Gene mumbled.

After hours of practice, the rest of the group showed little improvement. Ben didn't have another throw quite as good as his first one, but he did manage to hit at least one of the targets three times and caught the Battlerang every time it returned.

Finally Bridgit called for an end to the practice. She informed them that the mission was to set out in three weeks' time and that practice would be intense until then.

"Hey, do you guys want to grab a bite? I'm starving." Nora the leprechaun rubbed her tiny stomach for emphasis. Everyone agreed except for Gene, who, giving Ben a sour look, excused himself and went back to the intern dorms. Jeannie followed after him, but as she said good-bye to her friends, Ben thought she seemed slightly less cold than she had before.

"What did I do to make Gene so mad at me?" Ben wondered aloud.

Jonathan chuckled. "Don't worry about it. He's that way with all humans. Give old Purple-butt some time and he'll get used to you. Besides"—Jonathan gave Ben a meaningful look—"you'd be pretty grumpy, too, if you were the only Jinn in recent history that had been born without an ounce of magical ability."

As Ben considered this, the group rounded an ancient-looking brick building and proceeded down an alleyway. They were soon at a very ordinary green door labeled in small golden letters, THE POT O' GOLD. But the inside of the restaurant was the farthest thing from ordinary that Ben had ever seen.

CHAPTER TWENTY

The Pot o' Gold

*B*en's eyes boggled as he gazed around the immense dining room, his mouth hanging slightly open. The ceiling looked like a blue sky after a summer rainstorm. The ground was covered with fresh-smelling clover, and the tables were made from immense tree stumps. A line of people stood near a long, sparkling, rainbow countertop that stretched from the sky and ended at a large black kettle. A gnarly old leprechaun was perched on a high chair above the cauldron, ladling something glittering into the bowls of the waiting customers.

"Whoa," Ben said, awestruck.

"Come on, let's get in line. It's pretty busy tonight," Jonathan said.

As the line snaked to the front, Ben smiled inwardly. The reality of where he was was slowly sinking in. Soon they neared the front of the line. Jonathan turned to him.

"When you get up to the guy at the pot, just wish for what you want to eat and it will appear in your bowl."

"Do I say it out loud, or just to myself?" Ben asked, thinking about the rules regarding birthday wishes.

"Out loud. This isn't powerful magic."

It was Jonathan's turn to order. He shouted up to the leprechaun, "Fish and chips, with extra ketchup on the side." The little old man grunted and dipped the immense ladle into the pot. "Oh, and could you add a Flooper Fizz[19] to that?"

The leprechaun looked irritated, but nodded. He pulled

---

[19] Flooper Fizz is the soft drink of choice for most young people at the Factory, mostly due to the ingenious advertising campaign by the company that produces it, Warburgle Incorporated. The catchy jingle, "Floop, floop, poopy-doop, fizz baby, yeah, yeah, yeah," proved to be so insanely catchy that nobody in the company could stop singing it. Unfortunately, this eventually led to the complete annihilation of Warburgle Inc., the first business ever to fail due to insanity. The production of future batches of Flooper Fizz was later taken over by a small group of hearing-impaired leprechauns.

the ladle from the cauldron and poured a glittering substance into Jonathan's bowl. It shimmered there for a moment, then transformed to a delicious-looking platter of fish and chips.

Ben must have been staring too long, because the old leprechaun cleared his throat agitatedly.

"Hurry up, laddie, I haven't got all day!"

Ben was so overwhelmed and distracted, he couldn't think of what to order. "I'll have the same as what he had."

In moments his bowl was filled with the same glittering substance, and as it transformed, the smell of the golden fried fish filled his nostrils. His stomach growled hungrily in response.

"Oi, Ben! Over here." Nora stood on the group's table centerpiece, a large, wooden harp, and waved to Ben. Ben carried his tray to the table carefully and sat down.

"So what do you guys think of O'Reilly? She's a real trip, huh?" Jonathan asked, his mouth full of crispy fish.

Fizzle replied, "Yeah, I've never seen anybody throw like that. I bet she's even better than Candlewick."

"No way." Nora paused between bites of her cheeseburger to comment. She turned to Ben, who was so focused on his food that he hadn't been paying attention. "What did you think of her, Ben? You were the only one who impressed her, after all."

Ben looked up, momentarily surprised. "What? Oh, well, this is all pretty new to me, so I don't know who to even compare her with, y'know?"

He paused to finish a bite of salty french fry, then glanced up at his new friends, his skin prickling with embarrassment.

"I've never been very good at sports." He took a drink of the sparkling soft drink to hide his blushing face. Fizzle responded with a smile.

"Well, you were certainly good today. In fact, you were better than good; you were fantastic."

Ben felt happy for the first time since he had gained the power to make his wishes come true on earth. Although the prospect of going to some kind of war with an enemy straight out of a video game filled him with apprehension, he thought the whole thing would be a lot easier with his newfound friends by his side.

"Wait until Candlewick finds out about Ben's throw. He's gonna go crazy." The others at the table laughed at Jonathan's remark. Ben looked up.

"Why?"

Nora took a drink of her soda pop and grinned. "Mr. Candlewick is a Battlerang fanatic. He practices constantly, loves the thing. He even had the idea of manufacturing

Battlerang toys for kids. Ones that weren't actually weapons."
She rolled her eyes as if this were a ridiculous idea. Ben was
confused.

"Well, back on earth we have something similar called a
boomerang. It was considered a weapon once, but now you
can even buy one in a toy store. It sounds like a fun idea to
me."

Fizzle shot Ben a curious look. "You know, it's funny.
You're a lot like him, you know?" She smiled. "I remember
when he was around your age, brand-new to Wishworks.
My mother worked here at the Factory, and I used to come
around and visit her often." She paused, reflecting. "He loved
carrying around a spare Battlerang in his hip pocket. 'Just in
case,' he always said."

Ben was amazed. Fizzle only looked a few years older
than he, but she was old enough to remember Candlewick
way back then? Fizzle read his expression and chuckled.

"We fair folk age differently than you humans. I'll be 120
on my next birthday."

Ben's jaw dropped.

"Wow. I mean," he blushed furiously, "you don't look that
old to me."

She smiled playfully and threw a french fry at him. Ben
ducked and grinned broadly. He liked knowing he was a little

bit like Mr. Candlewick.

The small group stayed late at the table, well after the blue sky above their heads had turned to starry night. Leprechauns lit paper lanterns in the tree branches above their heads, and when they brought around the dessert tray, Ben helped himself to a decadent piece of chocolate cake. And then he helped himself to another.

= CHAPTER TWENTY-ONE =

The Ticking Clock

"**M**aster, the Curse-atina is just days away from completion," Simon Spinchley whined from his newly misshapen lips. He bowed deeply before the imposing figure who sat at a small harpsichord, deep in concentration.

Thornblood held up a finger as he penned a final line, and played a small bit of music on the ivory keyboard. He sat up with a satisfied smile, taking the parchment in his hands.

"Yes. That will do nicely." He turned and looked down at his cowering servant.

"See to it that it takes no longer."

Simon didn't dare lift his gaze from the flagstones, too terrified to look his evil overlord full in the face. After a moment, Thornblood's voice spoke lightly again.

"Go now, Simon. See to your duties. I am growing impatient."

"Yes, my liege."

Simon bowed deeply and turned, his insect legs clattering echoes in the cold stone hall.

Thornblood blotted the ink on the parchment with a sprinkle of sand and placed his feathered quill down.

He was ready for his concert performance.

≋ CHAPTER TWENTY-TWO ≋

A Near Miss

"**T**hrowing the Battlerang in formation is one of the most effective ways to insure that you connect with several targets at once." Ms. O'Reilly pointed at the blackboard drawing behind her, which illustrated the battle plan. "But it requires a lot of practice and, unfortunately, time is not on our side. I don't expect that you will be able to get this one right away, but let's go outside to the landing field and give it a try."

Ben moved with the group to the waiting field. Sure enough, word had reached Candlewick about Ben's first day of training, and Candlewick had been to see Ben that morning before practice. He had clapped Ben on the shoulder and ruffled his hair, talking excitedly about how much fun he had learning to throw at his age, and he had even given Ben a few tips for practice, promising to come watch him throw when he could get away from the office.

"Please line up shoulder to shoulder, but not too close. You should have enough room for your arm to throw between you and the person next to you."

A powerful shoulder pushed Ben roughly to the side. He eyed Gene reproachfully. He had been carefully avoiding contact with the husky Jinn and wished he had chosen a different place to stand.

His thoughts were interrupted by Ms. O'Reilly's shout. "When I blow the whistle, everyone throw at once. Ready?"

They nodded. A whistle blew. Battlerangs flew into the air at crazy angles. Ben noticed with some pride that his made the most graceful arc. He was also the only one who caught his own throw.

Gene glanced at him disgustedly. "Show-off."

Ben didn't say anything. Ms. O'Reilly complimented the effort and gave some constructive criticism before the next try.

FWEEET! Again, Ben was elbowed hard by Gene and

crashed to the ground before he could throw. Gene then released his own Battlerang.

"You gotta be more careful on the wet grass, short stuff." Gene leered at Ben.

But Ben spotted something that Gene couldn't see. The Battlerang that the Jinn had thrown was rocketing back toward him, glowing with deadly white heat. If Ben didn't do something it would . . .

CRACK! Ben expertly aimed a throw at the rocketing Battlerang and splintered the weapon in midair just as it was about to collide with the back of Gene's head. When Gene realized what had happened, he sat down on the springy turf with a loud *thud.*

"What did I tell you about never taking your eyes off your throw?" Ms. O'Reilly looked furious. Gene, turning a very pale shade of purple, nodded his head mutely.

As the group packed up their Battlerangs and gear, Ben was surprised to see a purple hand offered to him as he knelt by his bag. Gene looked uncomfortable and avoided eye contact.

"Hey, I . . . uh . . . sorry about giving you such a hard time, Piff. Thanks for what you did back there."

The Jinn's apology took Ben by surprise. He shook the offered hand.

"No problem," Ben said.

Gene nodded and walked away. Ben watched the hulking boy disappear inside the long training building.

Jonathan Pickles's voice sounded from over Ben's shoulder. "Wow, I never thought I'd see that happen. Ol' Purple-butt offering an apology!" He shook his head wonderingly.

≋ ≋ ≋

The next two weeks passed quickly. Ben's aptitude with the Battlerang was the talk of the Factory, and he often had seasoned Wishworks Warriors attending the practice sessions just to watch him throw. He had even adopted the habit of carrying an extra Battlerang in his hip pocket.

The only part of the training that Ben was not doing well in was in flying the Battle Chairs. The group had a very old instructor named Bernhard O'Malley, a leprechaun who had flown with the Four-Leaf Clover Squadron in the Great Wishworks War.[20] Ben had a hard enough time with flying when it was supposedly safe. When he thought about people in the sky trying to shoot each other down, his fear was so great that his knees went all wobbly.

---

[20] Bernhard O'Malley was the most decorated leprechaun in the war and is now over one thousand years old.

"Aw, it's not that bad," Jonathan Pickles, taking his turn at the gunner position, called back to Ben. Ben frowned and stared at the blinking dashboard lights with trepidation.

"I've got a fear of heights, okay?" snapped Ben. "I'm not like you guys. It's easy for you."

"Just relax and you'll be fine," Jonathan said confidently.

Ben nodded and tried to calm his fluttering stomach. He had learned to trust his new friend's flying abilities, but it still didn't make the takeoffs and landings any easier for him.

A uniformed pilot motioned with signal flags that they were to take off. Ben gulped and pressed the pedal under his right foot, engaging the flapping wings, and then slowly pulled back on the control stick.

Ben followed the other chairs in close formation, keeping his eyes locked on his position and his knuckles white on the stick. Jonathan, who loved flying more than anything else, tried to refrain from his usual excited chatter, instead keeping his voice steady and encouraging as Ben followed the other chairs in the long loop around the airfield.

"Now don't panic, but we're gonna take it in for a landing." Jonathan's voice was reassuring, but Ben felt his heart leap into his throat.

"Jon, no! I don't think I can."

"Trust me. You can do it. Look, I'll be right here if

anything goes wrong and can take over, okay?"

Ben's hand shook as he took the control stick and prepared to land.

"Easy, easy . . . that's it. We're almost down."

Ben watched the ground rise up much more quickly than he had anticipated. Panicking, he pulled back on the stick, sending the chair flapping upward in a manic ascent.

"Whoa! I said easy!" Jon shouted.

Ben eased the stick back forward, leveling the chair off once more.

The older boy chuckled. "Don't be so jittery; the chair will do the work for you. Now, let's try it again."

Ben nodded, his lips pressed together in a white line as the chair circled once more for an approach to the landing field. He eased the stick forward and had the sinking feeling in his stomach as the chair settled into its descent.

"That's it, you've got it . . . Nice!"

The wings of the chair shuddered as the chair set down on the grassy field. The landing was a little bumpy, but the lesson had gone better than Ben had expected.

"See! What did I tell ya?" Jonathan Pickles slapped Ben on the back as he emerged from the cockpit.

It was terrifying, but he had done it. Ben hoped that by some miracle he would find a way to be less nervous when he had to do the whole thing over again.

Next time, he thought, *it'll be for real*.

CHAPTER TWENTY-THREE

The Big Day

The morning dawned with clear blue skies. Ben had been awake for several hours, nursing an unsettled stomach and rubbing his bleary eyes. All of his dreams the night before had been flying dreams, in which he kept plummeting to the earth and crashing onto a hard, rocky floor. He felt grumpy and miserable as he threw on his freshly pressed Wishworks flight suit and tied his sneakers.

After shoving his favorite Battlerangs into his back pocket, he stumbled down the stony path to the Wing and a Prayer Café.

A long line of employees snaked out of the main entrance, but he soon spotted Nora, who waved him over to a spot where she and Fizzle stood in line.

"Morning, Ben." The tiny leprechaun surveyed him with a critical glance. "You look awful. What did you do, lose your comb?" She playfully indicated Ben's unruly hair.

"Where's Jon?" He scanned the crowd, searching for him.

"Allergies. He can't go up," Fizzle said sadly. "Candlewick said the pressure on his ears would be too dangerous. He was really bummed about it, too. He has been looking forward to this for weeks."

Ben swallowed hard. He and Jonathan were a team. Having a friend that he could trust had been the one thing that had given him enough courage to go up in the flying chairs. He wondered nervously who he would be paired with in the upcoming battle.

The line wound its way to the front and the two girls placed their orders. Ben, despite Nora's encouragement to eat something, refused. His stomach flip-flopped much too awkwardly, anticipating the dangerous day to come.

"I think I've figured out what I'm gonna do when I capture the Wish Globe," Ben whispered.

Nora paused between bites of her pancakes. "Yeah, what?"

"I was thinking. Why couldn't I really quickly wish for my parents back and *then* wish for the globe to be destroyed? That would work, right?"

Fizzle was silent for a moment before replying. "I don't know if you can make that kind of wish. I think there are some kind of limits on bringing dead people back, y'know?"

Nora swallowed her bite and replied. "Besides, it's gonna be really hard to even get into Curseworks. The place is crawling with horrible guards." The little leprechaun cut another slice of pancake. "Once you get the globe, you probably won't even have time to think about it. Remember, you have to escape with the globe outside of the Curseworks walls before you can use it."

Ben considered this. But he still couldn't put the plan out of his mind. Would it be possible? Maybe if he was really specific in how he made the wish . . .

As the girls chatted in low tones about the upcoming battle, Ben stared out the large plate-glass window overlooking the landing field. Several crew people were busily making last-minute checks on the Battle Chairs. One of the crewmen motioned for his small son, who had been watching from a distance, to join him at the chair. The boy's mother nodded her approval, and the little boy rushed over to where his daddy stood. The father grinned and lifted his son into the cockpit. The boy waved through the glass to his mother, smiling broadly and revealing two missing front teeth. Ben's throat tightened as he watched the happy family.

I have to try.

After finishing their meal and replacing their breakfast trays, the friends walked from the Wing and a Prayer Café to the large hangar where stadium-style seats had been erected for Candlewick's last-minute mission briefing. When Ben got to his section, his stomach sank. Sitting in the chair marked *Pilot* was Gene.

Great. The Jinn gave Ben a curt nod. Although things hadn't been quite as nasty between them since Ben had rescued the older boy during Battlerang practice, they had carefully kept their distance from each other, avoiding any potential conflict.

And now I have to trust this guy as he flies us hundreds of feet above the ground, Ben realized. This morose thought was interrupted by Candlewick's voice echoing over a PA system.

"Can everybody hear me?" Murmurs of "yes" and "no" rumbled through the crowd.

Candlewick continued. "Ladies and gentlemen, if I could draw your attention to the center screen." He indicated a large projection screen hovering behind the stage. "Warren,

Wallace, and Wimbledon have returned from their latest foray into Curseworks and have reports on Thornblood's military progress."

The scratchy black-and-white film depicted hideous Spider Monkeys, some riding immense wormlike beasts towing black catapults, and others carrying elaborate battering rams with iron heads like monstrous dragons. The horde howled war chants as they marched through the lands west of the Wishworks Factory.

Candlewick spoke while the film commenced. "It is my unfortunate duty to inform you that Simon Spinchley Snifflewiffle is now counted among their numbers."

There were startled gasps and a few cries of disbelief. A new image flickered onto the screen: a small black orb resting on a splintered tabletop in a gray, dripping dungeon. From somewhere off to the right, there was a terrific blast of light and the orb burst into flame. Flickering fire danced for a moment, casting weird shadows on the wall before morphing into something else entirely. Ben stared, horrified, as a scaly, dragonlike monster emerged, its eyes glowing with pure hatred.

"What you are witnessing is the transformation of an ordinary curse into a creature capable of bringing down an entire Wishworks squadron. Adolfus Thornblood has invented a machine powered by the Unlimited Wish Globe.

Ben felt a sense of deep guilt. That was *his* wish inside the globe.

"This machine," Candlewick continued, "can magnify a curse's power to unthinkable dimensions." The film stopped and the house lights came back up.

"Thanks to the magical prowess of several Jinns, we have been able to outfit our pilots with curse-proof shields on their Battle Chairs. We are fairly confident that the shields can effectively deter three or four attacks by the creatures, but we can't be sure they will last longer than that." Candlewick paused. "The aerial battle will be extremely difficult. I have enlisted the help of the Lucky Pennies,[21] one of our finest and most experienced squadrons, to accompany our new pilots into battle." There was a slight smattering of applause. "I'll be leading the squadron myself, with the company of Bernhard O'Malley." More surprised whispers erupted through the room at this news.

---

[21] Penelope Thicklepick, president of Wishworks (1898–1912), was nicknamed "Lucky Penny" by her fellow flying officers for her exceptional flying abilities and Battlerang skills. She also seemed to possess an endless supply of good fortune on the battlefield and was rumored to have glued a penny on top of her Battlerang, claiming that it brought her extra luck when aiming for a hard-to-hit target. The practice of gluing a penny on a Battlerang was later adopted by the entire Lucky Penny Squadron, and remains in use to this day.

Candlewick continued. "While the main force defends the Factory from the invading Spider Monkeys, the aerial force will sneak behind enemy lines for a surprise attack, rejoining the main forces behind the Wishworks gates upon accomplishment of the mission."

Motioning for the projector to be turned off, he waited, looking into several of the assembled faces before he broke the tension-filled silence.

"Ladies and gentlemen, the time has come. The war we are about to fight is not just to protect our lives and loved ones, but, more importantly, everything that Wishworks stands for." Candlewick walked out from behind the podium and into the assembled crowd.

"This war that we fight is to protect our reason for living, the reason we get up in the morning, and the reason we can peacefully return to our beds at night." Candlewick shared a brief smile with the warriors; his face was relaxed and glowing with confidence. "The very thing that Thornblood seeks to destroy is the same thing that gives us the courage to stand against him. Wishes are nothing more than the embodiment of hope itself. Hope for healing. Hope for a better day. Hope that what tomorrow brings will help us get a little bit closer to true happiness." He paused next to the row of interns and gripped each of their shoulders, ending the last part of his speech in front of Ben and Gene.

"It is hope, my friends, that will bring us victory."

Candlewick walked back to the podium to an eruption of applause. Someone in the assembly struck up the chorus of an old battle song from the time of the Great Wishworks War. It was a moving song, and Ben felt encouraged as the singers' voices faded under renewed shouts of "Victory!"

≋ ≋ ≋

Moments later, in the hangar holding the Battle Chairs, Ben watched with a fluttering stomach as a Factory employee dumped a large bucket of cannonballs into the hopper mounted upon a chair's flank.

Gene's voice came from behind Ben. "It's okay to feel nervous."

"I'm not nervous," Ben lied.

"I've seen you up there with Pickles. Don't worry, I'm an even better pilot than he is. We'll be fine," the Jinn said.

Ben looked doubtful. He hadn't paid close attention to the Jinn's piloting skills during practice because he was too busy concentrating on making it back down to the ground alive.

There was only one thing that Ben could think of that brought him any comfort at all, and that was the plan for his final wish once he captured the globe. It was the only hope he had of ever seeing his parents again, and it was a strong motivator for getting back into the air.

"Two minutes. Pilots and gunners to your chairs," a voice announced.

Gene motioned for Ben to follow. "It's time! Let's go!"

The words WHAT GOES AROUND were illustrated in flowing script on one side of the flying machine, with the follow-up statement, COMES AROUND, on the other. Jonathan had commissioned the artwork for the chair, intending it to encourage Ben's Battlerang abilities, but the way Ben felt right now, he would be surprised if he could raise his shaking arm to even throw!

Ben climbed into the cockpit and took the seat behind the pilot's chair. Gene followed, and they both put on their gauntlets and protective goggles.

The chairs were ushered onto the landing field by several crewmen. Moments later the signal rang for takeoff. Ben saw out the rear window some of his other friends start the flapping wings of their chairs. Nora and Fizzle flew together. Fizzle had proven herself to be a competent pilot, having flown all of her life, and Nora was passable with the Battlerang as long as her temper didn't flare up when she missed a shot.

Ben watched as Jeannie gripped the controls of a Battle

Chair next to his, her usually healthy purple face now a nervous shade of lavender. Another intern that he had seen once or twice before sat behind her as gunner. The boy leprechaun caught Ben's eye and gave him an encouraging thumbs-up. Ben smiled back weakly.

"Roger that, tower," Gene said into the receiver. Then the chair started to shudder under the powerful strokes of its giant wings.

Ben's stomach lurched as the chair ascended rapidly into the sky, leaving the landing field far below in just seconds. He ground his teeth together in an effort to keep from throwing up. With a roar of wings, the Lucky Penny Squadron appeared to Ben's left. Thomas Candlewick, leading the squad, gave him a salute through the window.

Ben raised a gloved hand and returned the salute, forcing himself to smile.

Just think about Mom and Dad. Get this over with and you'll see them again.

Gene banked the Battle Chair and flew into formation with the Lucky Pennies. The first phase of the mission had begun.

CHAPTER TWENTY-FOUR

The Enemy at the Gates

Perkins struggled with the belt that fastened his golden breastplate around his rotund middle. He hadn't put on the armor that all Wishworks employees wear during their obligatory six months of army training in quite a while.

"Ooogh." He groaned as he managed to get the very last hole in the belt through the buckle. The armor was tight, but he wouldn't have dreamed of going into battle without it. He examined himself in the mirror, sucking in his belly as much as he could.

Candlewick had informed him the night before that he, Perkins, would be the one to lead the charge. Perkins was surprised. Historically, the president of the Factory led the attack,[22] but Candlewick felt that he needed to watch over Ben and make sure that nothing went wrong.

Perkins understood. The stakes had never been so high. He gazed at his reflection and adjusted his glasses, trying to look fierce and commanding.

It just didn't work.

"Excuse me, sir." The knock at the door startled him out of his pose.

"Enter."

The young intern, breathless and pale, stood at attention and saluted.

"Your attention is needed, sir. The walls are being breached."

Perkins looked out the window to the field outside the Factory. In the far distance, behind the empty tower that once housed all of the Feathered Funicula chairs, a long, dark, ominous cluster of bodies was moving. Perkins squinted and

---

[22] There is only one other instance of a president not leading the charge into battle. Bertram Snicklepants (1827–1898) was prevented from going into battle due to the fact that his immense bulk would not fit into a Battle Chair. After the war, he commissioned a large winged sofa to be built so that he would not be placed in such an awkward position ever again.

could make out the bloodred banners of the Curseworks Factory whipping in the cloudless sky.

"I want every Battlerang thrower on the field immediately! We don't have any time to lose!"

The boy saluted once more and backed out the door. Perkins picked up his Battlerang from the desk, placed it in its leather holster, and examined himself once more.

"Oh, well," he muttered. "Looks aren't everything."

≈ Chapter Twenty-Five ≈

Dogfight!

"**P**ull up, PULL UP!" Ben shouted. The hideous creature hovering in front of him leered as it drew its dragonish head level with the window.

There had been a mysterious flash of red, and then seemingly from nowhere a wave of terrible curses had flown at them, screeching with frenzied delight. They pounded against the squadron of chairs, spitting a horrible green acid that would have burned right through the windshield if it hadn't been magically curse-proofed.

But as soon as the curses realized that the windshields

repelled their attacks, they directed their foul burning acid at the connecting joints of the Battle Chair wings. Ben had watched, horrified, as more than one of the chairs plummeted to the ground with their severed wings trailing behind them.

Candlewick's voice crackled over the speakers, startling Ben back to the present.

"Watch out, Ben, you've got one coming in at four o'clock!"

Before Ben had time to think about where four o'clock was, a fat, black, scaly curse smashed against the curse-proof window. It howled and reared its head, ready to spit its fiery acid on the flying chair.

Gene responded quickly, jerking back on the stick and whipping the Battle Chair into a steep ascent. Ben's heart pounded. He could see the curse directly below, following them rapidly.

Ben leaned out the window and reached for his Battlerang. Focusing on the curse and timing his throw, he wheeled back and hurled his weapon.

The throw went wide and the curse reacted quickly, dodging the toss and accelerating upward at renewed speed. As the Battlerang made its wide arc and landed back in Ben's outstretched hand, Gene called out.

"Hang on! I'm gonna try to lose him!"

Ben's stomach leaped to his throat as the chair went into a spiral spin and rocketed toward the ground. The beast that chased them careened out of the way to avoid the hurtling chair but then recovered, shooting a spout of green acid from its fanged jaws directly at the pilot's window.

CRACKKK! The curse-proof shield crackled like lightning as the glowing green jet glanced harmlessly off the window's surface. Gene, sweat beading up on his temples, let out a bottled breath.

"That was close," he rasped. "Can you see him, Ben?"

All tension between Ben and Gene had disappeared under the urgency of battle. Ben craned his neck around the rear window. The curse had banked his turn and was rushing back at them, full force.

"He's coming back! I'm gonna try again," Ben shouted.

Ben leaned out around the protective glass and took aim once more. He reached back as far as he could and thrust the Battlerang forward.

It was a direct hit! The curse only had time to emit one terrified screech before the weapon sliced neatly through its middle, sending it spiraling down.

"Woohoo!" Gene let out a cry of delight. "You got him!"

Ben fell back into his chair, pale and shaking. He tried not to think about what was really happening. *It's just target practice. Just like on the ground. Don't think about it.* He repeated this over and over to himself.

≋ ≋ ≋

The battle raged on. Ben and Gene flew with the squadron over the forest that stood between Wishworks and Curseworks.

"It's an ambush!" Gene cried as he spotted a new horde of curses, these twice as large as the one they had fought before.

The remaining interns rushed to the attack, flanked by the more experienced Lucky Pennies pilots. The young pilots flew well, doing their best to match the expert acrobatics of their more seasoned guardians. Ben estimated that out of the one hundred Battle Chairs that had flown into battle, fewer than fifty remained. He only hoped that his friends were still alive.

Battle Chairs darted up and down in the cloudless sky, wings flapping furiously, the flying curses chasing right behind. Battlerangs, glowing with white-hot intensity, stood out against the vibrant blue, whirling through the air like shooting stars. Ben watched, horrified, as one of the Battle Chairs from the Lucky Pennies Squadron was hit by enemy fire and lost its wings, falling to the ground like a stone.

"I've got one coming in at twelve o'clock! I'll get you a clear shot!" Gene shouted.

Ben held his breath as the curse swept into view. When the curse was in range, Ben reared back and threw his Battlerang. There was a pause and then an answering scream of anguish from somewhere off to his left.

"Got him!" Gene's exultant cry was cut short, however, when two bolts crashing into the front of the chair met the magical shield and rattled the cockpit.

"That's it for the shield." The chair spun and swooped upward. From his vantage point, Ben couldn't find the source of the attack.

"Uh-oh, they're coming right at us!" Gene yelled. "Ben, quick, use your . . . Wait a sec . . . YEAH!" Gene swerved the chair and Ben caught a glimpse of Candlewick's chair, having just saved their necks by taking down two massive enemy curses, rocketing through the fiery smoke that was left behind. Ben briefly saw a grinning Candlewick flash him the thumbs-up sign before he flew out of sight.

In spite of being outnumbered, the expert pilots of the Lucky Pennies Squadron chased the enemy down, Battlerangs blazing.

Ben saw Nora and Fizzle closing in on the last of the creatures. Suddenly, in a surprise maneuver, the curse did a loop and spouted acid directly at the front window of the two girls' rapidly gaining Battle Chair.

There was a tremendous explosion and the chair careened under the force of the blast, coming directly at Ben and Gene.

WHOOOOOMMMMP! Everything went black for a moment, then the spinning force of gravity pulled Ben's face tight against his skull. The impact of the chair collision had knocked them into a downward spiral, and glass shards were everywhere!

"Gene! Pull up!"

The wings of the chair weren't moving, and the ground was rushing toward them at an impossible speed. Ben struggled to crane his neck around and check on Gene. The Jinn was slumped in his chair, his forehead bleeding.

Without thinking, Ben scrambled to the cockpit. He grabbed the controls frantically and tried to remember the operating instructions he'd been taught. "I can't do this! I can't do this!" he heard himself screaming as he searched the rows of senseless buttons and switches for a solution. The ground was getting closer and closer by the second.

At the last possible second, Ben pulled up on the stick and shoved his feet hard into the pedal releasing the air brakes. With a groaning scream, the wings leaped back to life, and the Battle Chair swooped over the tops of the trees, shearing off a few of the closest branches.

In moments Ben had landed the machine in an emergency landing field. Candlewick and the other interns ran to the chair as it fluttered to a stop. "He needs help."

Ben gasped and felt the world around him spinning. Moments later he felt as if he were looking through a camera lens as it slowly shut, the shouting voices around him growing faint. The world faded away as his head slumped against the smoldering console.

CHAPTER TWENTY-SIX

The Wishworks War

*I*t had happened without a warning of any kind. A booming noise, like huge hands playing the bottom keys of a massive pipe organ, shook the air. The terrified Wishworks employees stopped what they were doing as the ground trembled beneath their feet. There was a momentary hush and then Perkins paled as he watched a bloodred bolt pierce the sky, accompanied by horrific organ music.

The sound of hundreds of unearthly screams split the air. In moments, a torrent of wailing creatures came hurtling toward the Wishworks wall. Their worst fears had been confirmed. Thornblood's Curse-atina had been completed!

Galvanized into action, Perkins shouted to the troops.

"Battlerangs to the ready! I want men on every one of those walls, on the double!"

In moments the Battlerangs flew in formation like a flock of deadly eagles, cutting down the seemingly endless swarm of twisted creatures that lifted rickety ladders, attempting to scale the Factory walls.

"The left flank! The left!" Perkins shouted to the commander in front of him from atop his tall golden platform.

The commander responded quickly, sounding a curved horn and leading his troops out from a hidden Factory tunnel. The troops charged to the left of the field outside the walls where a particularly large group of Spider Monkeys were using a battering ram to crush through the Wishworks main gate.

The battle turned fierce as the creatures broke through the gates, but to Perkins's immense relief, the tactics that Candlewick had left for him were working. The Spider Monkeys attacked with wild abandon, screaming and thrusting their magic curse-covered spears wildly, leaping over the crumpled forms of their comrades and scuttling like locusts. The Wishworks army attacked with clockwork regularity, keeping to their ranks, and when the Battlerangs were thrown, the swordsmen advanced, cutting a swath before them.

At first the fight had seemed fairly even, but as it went on, the Wishworks Army gained strength. If the tide of battle continued this way, there was a good chance that they could win by the end of the day.

Then the skirl of a bagpipe split the air, announcing the arrival of Warren, Wallace, and Wimbledon. The brass men, with their sword blades whirling in a mechanical dance, advanced into a large cluster of Spider Monkeys.

There were howls of rage and pain as the Spider Monkeys fell beneath the onslaught. Then, from a hidden corner of the battlefield, a troop of massive Jinns swinging giant scimitars swept through the evil forces on the right, blasting through the spidery creatures like sickles cutting down wheat.

≋ ≋ ≋

"What happened?" Ben was groggy and disoriented. He felt a reassuring hand on his shoulder and the face of Thomas Candlewick came into focus.

"A lot, actually." Candlewick looked grave. "While you were out we saw a horde of curses turn and fly into the Factory. Some of them are probably on earth by now, as well."

Ben grew quiet, feeling guilty.

"Is Gene okay?"

Candlewick nodded. "Yes, he's going to be all right. He's been flown to the hospital wing at the Factory." Ben was relieved. Candlewick paused a moment, searching for the right words.

"You did a pretty amazing thing back there, Ben." Ben looked up to see Candlewick smiling gently down at him. "You know, you're quite a kid. I deal with a lot of people and their wishes all the time, and well, I guess . . ."

He paused, looking out at the forest edge.

"I guess that if I ever met someone who deserved a wish for unlimited wishes to come true, it would be you." Candlewick laid a hand on Ben's shoulder. "You've got a lot of courage."

Ben smiled and shook his head. "Well, I sure didn't feel courageous." He looked up at Candlewick. "When I was back home, I went a little crazy with the whole wish thing. I don't blame you for thinking I was some kind of a jerk."

Candlewick chuckled and tousled Ben's hair. "If we get through this in one piece, we need to talk some more. We have pretty similar backgrounds, you and I."

Candlewick helped Ben to his feet and they walked over to where the rest of the troops waited. Ben was relieved to see that Nora, Fizzle, and Jeannie were okay. The female Jinn gave Ben a warm smile, the first that he had ever received from her. Ben smiled back, sensing that things would be different between him and both of the Jinns from now on.

Nora had her arm in a sling, but she and Fizzle were otherwise unharmed. The quick-thinking fairy had used her magic pixie dust to cushion the impact of the Battle Chair before it crashed. They beamed at Ben as he approached, and Fizzle kissed him on the cheek.

Candlewick asked a senior officer of the Lucky Pennies for a damage report.

"Well, sir, we lost five more, and two of the Battle Chairs are out of commission." The sergeant looked concerned.

Candlewick did some mental calculation. "With Gene gone, I'll be flying with Ben the remaining five miles to Curseworks. Sergeant, I want you to lead the rest of the force on a diversion. By now the word has reached Thornblood that we are out here, and we need to keep him off our tail." Candlewick ran a hand through his gray hair. "With a little luck, he won't notice a single chair on its way to the fortress."

The sergeant saluted. In moments the squadron Battle Chairs were started and flew in formation off to the east.

Ben was surprised that he didn't feel nervous this time

as he settled himself into the gunner's seat. Perhaps having such a close brush with death had changed something inside of him.

His nerves were steady as the chair fluttered to life under Candlewick's expert guidance and rose into the starlit sky—a fluttering shadow hoping to pass unnoticed by the Curseworks guards.

≋ Chapter Twenty-Seven ≋
The Seven O'Clock News

"*G*ood evening, and welcome to Channel Five News at Seven." The anchorman, staring fixedly at the camera, recited his evening monologue. "I'm Terrence Blackwell."

The pretty coanchor next to him smiled. "And I'm Libby Sanchez, and this is a special report."

The anchorman turned to face camera two as a window with a digital graphic materialized behind him. The graphic showed people frozen mid-stride, running away from a giant question mark.

"Chaos reigned in Los Angeles today as panic over a mysterious phenomenon took place. We go live to Willard Winchell, who is at a shopping mall downtown."

A new reporter filled the screen. Behind him people screamed and ran through the mall.

"Thank you, Terrence. Here at the Los Angeles Shopping Center, people are complaining of all kinds of sudden misfortune." He passed the microphone to a gentleman standing next to him, whose face was stretched painfully into the shape of a huge silver coin. "Tell us what happened to you, sir."

The man, looking nervous, replied. "Well, all I said to my wife was, 'What d'ya think I am, made of money?' And then she gave me this real mean look." He gestured to his head. "The next thing I know . . . this happened."

The reporter then turned to a woman who stood beside him, sobbing uncontrollably.

"I know that my sister Jackie is somehow responsible for this; she always claimed that I was too nosy for my own good."

The woman's nose was huge, resembling a bumpy squash. Willard Winchell grimaced and laid a consoling hand on her shoulder. The woman broke into a fresh wave of hysterical sobs as the reporter turned back to the camera. "Dozens of similar reports like these and worse have been flooding the operators at 911." He removed a notebook and read from it. "Reports of people suddenly being stricken with horrible diseases and missing golf swings are all over the city." He closed the notebook and looked intently at the camera. "A teacher at a local elementary school found himself covered with a flesh-eating fungus and unable to say the word *homework*. A police officer in Portland, Oregon, started giving himself speeding tickets for no apparent reason. Unconfirmed reports say that many corporate executives have been changing into rats and slugs." The reporter shuffled through a small stack of index cards, then turned back to the camera. "The list goes on and on."

Libby Sanchez interrupted. "Do we know who or what is causing all of this?"

Willard Winchell shook his head. "Many are saying that the mass hysteria is some kind of psychic phenomenon caused by UFOs, allowing the terrible things we wish on our enemies to come true, but until we have more information, it is anybody's guess."

The camera went back to the newsroom, where Terrence nodded sagely offscreen. "Thank you, Will. Sounds really bad out there."

Libby interrupted, addressing Willard. "Is there a number

that people can call if they feel that they have fallen victim to this phenomenon?"

Terrence shot Libby a dirty look. She wasn't supposed to interrupt him during a report. He turned back to the camera and continued.

"In other news, a surfing parakeet named Bubbles made history today . . ."

Libby interrupted him again. "Excuse me, Terrence, but I think the people should know where they can call . . ."

Terrence's eyes glinted with malice as he forced a smile and spoke through gritted teeth.

"Zip it, Sanchez."

A large metal zipper appeared across the pretty coanchor's mouth. She emitted a muffled scream and shook her hands violently. The newsroom fell into chaos. Terrence pointed at the coanchor and laughed.

"Hey, everybody, look at Sanchez! She's—"

But he never got any further. Sanchez unzipped her mouth and cursed angrily, "Go suck an egg, Terrence!"

The anchorman froze for a moment under his coanchor's angry gaze and then let out muffled protests as an ostrich-size egg appeared in his mouth.

CHAPTER TWENTY-EIGHT

Stealing the Globe

Ben held the map in his trembling hand, sweat pouring into his eyes. The shaft that he had descended into led to the Curseworks furnace, and he knew that the turn that would lead him to the Curse-atina had to be coming up soon.

He had passed several unusual rooms during his harrowing descent. He'd sneaked past a room marked PROFANITY PRODUCTION and, in spite of the heavy walls, blushed when he heard the foul curses that were emanating from underneath a crack in the doorway in dark green gaseous clouds. Worming around another corner, he saw a room filled with evil-tempered black cats, broken glass, spilled salt, and bent horseshoes.

He turned the map that Candlewick had given him upside down and tried to get his bearings. The flight to Curseworks had gone perfectly: The usual guards were away, apparently enlisted as troops at the battlefront.

Ben could see that the turn was only about twenty feet ahead. He wondered what would have happened if a bigger kid had made this wish—there was no way that anyone larger than Ben could have ever squeezed down this narrow shaft.

Consulting the map once more, Ben noted that beyond the shaft was an iron grate. He went up to the grate, holding the map in his teeth. Peering through the bars, Ben saw sitting below him an ugly piece of machinery. It looked like a cross between an old pipe organ and some kind of medieval torture device.

Ben peered around, looking for guards, but there were none. *Thornblood probably figured that no one could sneak into his fortress,* Ben thought, *but he was wrong.*

Ben reached out and twisted the bars easily from their crumbling sockets and squeezed out the opening onto the flagstone floor.

He approached the machine cautiously. A piece of music

sat on a music stand, and Ben noticed that a faint, almost imperceptible screeching noise emitted from inside the rusted, weathered pipes. *That must be where the curses come out.*

He moved quietly around to the back of the machine. There, behind a tiny metal door, was the thing he was looking for—the globe. *His* globe.

It felt strange to see the thing that he had created, the globe that contained his own wish, sitting in front of his eyes. This was it. Once he was outside of the Curseworks walls, he could wish for his parents to come back, and then he would have everything he wanted. After that he would unwish his unlimited wish and fix everything back at Wishworks.

Reaching out cautiously, he touched the door that hid the precious globe.

"I wouldn't if I were you."

Ben wheeled around. Out of the shadows came Thornblood, his walking stick unsheathed to reveal a thin sword. Flanking him were three scuttling guards armed with evil-looking crossbows. Ben backed into the corner nearest the machine, his eyes darting around the room, looking for an escape.

The evil man tossed his top hat onto a nearby shelf and chuckled. "It is no use, boy. You might as well give up. I will never let you escape this room alive."

Ben stared at the cold, glowing eyes of the president. Mustering up his courage, he grabbed the Battlerang at his holster and whipped it as hard as he could at the elegantly clothed figure.

Expertly, Thornblood caught the spinning weapon in one of his delicate-looking hands and crushed it to bits.

"I'm surprised Candlewick sent a selfish boy like you on this mission." His thin lips twisted into a smirk. "He always was a very poor judge of character." Then his face took on a sympathetic expression.

"Ben, Ben, Ben." He smiled as he said this, like a teacher reprimanding a poor student. "You really don't understand what this is all about, do you?"

Ben replied angrily. "I know that you want to destroy the world with curses! Isn't that enough?"

Thornblood clucked his tongue and replied, "It is much more complicated than that. A curse is of far, far more importance than you realize. You, for one, should be especially interested in the importance of curses."

Ben hesitated at the door of the Wish Globe, feeling confused.

"Why?"

Thornblood smiled. "Where would the world be without

curses? From the smallest curse word to the greatest desire for your enemy's untimely demise, it is all about one simple thing."

Ben waited.

"Aw, c'mon, Ben. Don't know the answer? Well, I'll give it to you." He paused, then raised a finger skyward.

"Revenge."

Ben was puzzled. "What do you mean, revenge?"

Thornblood gestured widely. "Revenge, pure, sweet, and simple. Somebody does something to you, you get 'em back. You know, eye for an eye and all that! It is what makes the world go 'round, boy!" Thornblood's face glowed with passion. "It is what makes it all worthwhile! Seeing your enemy groveling at your feet, begging you for mercy." He gave Ben a shrewd look. "I'm sure that there are people in your own life that deserve to suffer, aren't there?"

Ben flashed to thoughts of Ms. Pinch and Mr. Roach. They had mistreated him from day one. Surely they deserved to get back what they had given him?

In spite of himself, he thought about how they deserved to feel like he had when he'd spent cold winter nights in the big dormitory room; when he had gone to bed hungry and when he had reeked from scrubbing out Mr. Roach's horrible pots.

Ben was so captivated by Thornblood's words that he didn't notice the villain motioning for the guards to advance.

"Yes, I can see by the look on your face that you have revenge in mind. You know, Ben"—Thornblood's voice turned soothing and friendly—"together we can take care of those people who were so mean to you. Just give me that little Wish Globe and we can make the whole thing fair. You deserve this, boy."

Ben hesitated. He knew it was wrong, but Thornblood's words were appealing. He was falling under Thornblood's spell.

He reached mechanically for the small, iron grate that held his Wish Globe. His head felt foggy, and deep inside he felt a cold, angry desire for revenge.

But just as he was about to open the door, a memory of his father flashed into his mind. Ben had been bullied at school by Jimmy Thompson and had emerged from the pushing match with skinned knees and a torn backpack. He sat on the bathroom counter while his dad sprayed Bactine on his scrapes. Ben could still feel the sting of the antiseptic on his scratches, and remembered telling his dad that he wished that Jimmy would be bitten by a thousand spiders. His dad had chuckled sympathetically and, as he placed a

Band-Aid on Ben's knee, said, "A famous man once said, 'Forgiveness is the sweetest revenge.'" He had looked up at Ben intently, measuring every word. "Do you know what he meant by that?"

Ben shook his head. His father smiled gently and continued.

"Hatred and wanting harm to come to your enemies will only make you miserable in the end. You have to learn to let it go, Ben. You give your enemies too much power when you allow them to eat you up inside."

The words now came into his heart like sunshine breaking through the clouds, forcing the cold rage that he had been feeling to disappear. His father was right. Forgiveness was all that mattered now.

After studying the globe for a full minute, he slowly turned to look at Thornblood, whose hold over Ben was lessening by the minute. Thornblood's impeccable suit was worn and frayed at the edges. The older man looked ravaged by the endless burden of harboring so much hate in his own soul. Thornblood didn't blink as he awaited Ben's decision. He obviously thought that he had Ben in the palm of his hand.

"Thanks for the offer, but I think I'll pass."

Thornblood's face registered shock, which quickly morphed into cold, icy rage. He raised his sword and advanced at Ben. Ben looked around desperately but saw no weapon in sight.

Suddenly, there was an ear-splitting whistle followed by a thunderous *BOOM!* as something huge collided with the balcony outside the darkened window. The walls shook and the floor trembled violently, causing loose mortar and stones to cascade around Ben, who almost dropped the delicate Wish Globe as he was thrown off balance.

Then, the last person Ben expected to see staggered through the ragged opening in the stone wall. A battered Candlewick, surrounded by golden light, stepped from the crashed remains of his Battle Chair.

"Right on time." Candlewick held out his hand to reveal a magic pocket watch, the source of the intense glow. The evil president, momentarily distracted, wheeled around at Candlewick.

"You!" His voice dripped with venom.

"Yes, me." Candlewick cocked his head and smiled lopsidedly. "Nice speech." He leaned back against the wall, a fixed grin on his face. "Boy, you sure can hold a grudge, can't you? I guess you're still upset because I laid you off." He paused, considering. "I still say that you were the worst intern Wishworks ever had."

Thornblood bellowed with rage and rushed at

Candlewick. Candlewick, seizing the opportunity, shouted, "BEN, NOW!"

Ben grabbed the globe. Out of the corner of his eye, he saw Thornblood slice his sword deeply into Candlewick's side.

Ben cried out, stunned. He had to act. He had to get the globe outside of the wish-proof walls of Curseworks so that he could make everything right again. Ben closed his hand around the Wish Globe and dashed around Thornblood, scrambling into the vent opening.

The Curseworks president's voice boomed after him, calling to the Spider Monkeys. "Don't let him get away!"

Ben had barely made it thirty feet inside the tunnel when the clicking of insect feet rattled behind him. Panicked, he struggled up the chamber as quickly as he could. Tears burned his eyes as he climbed, feeling waves of guilt about abandoning Candlewick, but also knowing that everything was up to him now. Forcing himself to place one scraped and battered elbow after the next, he climbed up the long tunnel to the roof.

As the hairy, groping claws brushed against his ankle, Ben emerged on top of the Curseworks tower and ran for the waiting Battle Chair.

But thousands of crawling, spidery bodies emerged from

every possible crack in the castle walls, rushing at Ben. Their insectine bodies glittered in the murky light. Ben raced for the chair, his heart pounding wildly as the clattering legs rattled over the uneven stones. Just a few more steps and he would be there!

A strong set of pincerlike hands grabbed his ankle. He kicked back as hard as he could. His foot made contact with a satisfied thud. There was a short, angry scream, and the grip loosened.

He dove into the cockpit and scrambled to right himself. Without warning, a powerful burning sensation seared his left arm, forcing him to drop the globe.

The magical curse-covered arrow, shot by one of the Spider Monkeys, took effect immediately, and Ben was suddenly consumed with agonizing pain. Liquid fire coursed through his veins, and he let out a tormented scream.

The first of the scuttling Spider Monkeys made a rush for the globe that was now rolling near the bottom of the Battle Chair. Ben, fighting through his haze of pain, lunged and made a desperate grab for the precious wish, but it was too late. The leering beast snatched it with its hairy paw and held it triumphantly in the air. Ben noticed that it was the only twisted monkey with perfectly white teeth. If only he had something to throw . . .

Seconds later Ben's spare Battlerang whistled through the air, knocking the globe out of Simon's startled grasp. In the desperate escape from Thornblood, he had forgotten about the spare that he always carried in his back pocket! Ben's arm burned with the effort of throwing the weapon.

In an instant he had scooped up the glowing ball and was hobbling as fast as he could back into the Battle Chair's cockpit.

Countless spidery bodies scuttled toward Ben, but he was already out of reach. Ben jerked hard on the control stick, and the Battle Chair's powerful wings flapped and rose into the air.

Enraged, the monkeys drew their crossbows and fired. *FLASH! CRACK!* With a crackle and a burning smell of ozone, the shields were gone! The chair spun wildly and the instrument panel flashed its red warning lights. The chair couldn't sustain a single direct hit or it would be all over!

Ben had barely time to think as the chair lurched and fell rapidly toward the ground. There was only time for one wish, only time to do the thing that mattered most. Barely clearing the wall, with the chair's wings flapping feebly, Ben grasped the globe with all of his might and concentrated on the words that he had rehearsed in his mind a million times.

I wish I had never made the wish for unlimited wishes.

CHAPTER TWENTY-NINE

A Final Wish

*B*en stood in Mr. Roach's darkened kitchen holding a smoking candle in one hand and a piece of chocolate birthday cake in the other. He noticed with a start that his arm didn't hurt anymore and quickly examined the place where the arrow had stung moments before. A sneering voice broke the silence.

"What did you wish for, Ben?"

The shadowy form of Mr. Roach stood exactly as it had before when Ben had been rooted to this very spot, feeling terrified.

This time it was different. Ben felt no fear. In fact, after what he had just been through, there was nothing that Mr. Roach could do to make him feel threatened ever again. Pausing a moment to consider this, he stared directly into Mr. Roach's eyes, his face calm and confident.

"I didn't wish for anything. I was hungry and I decided to have some of my cake."

Mr. Roach was stunned. Ben had never acted this way before! He surveyed Ben uncertainly in the darkness, a wary expression on his face. After a moment he replied.

"You realize that I will have to report this to Ms. Pinch."

"You can do that, but it won't make any difference." Ben stared Mr. Roach down. "I'm not afraid of either of you anymore. Go ahead, wake her up. I'm sure that she'll love being pulled out of bed in the middle of the night."

Ben turned his back on Mr. Roach, who stared in disbelief as he walked out the door and to the dormitory room. Once inside, he sat down on his army cot. He stared at the cake and candle in his hands.

A thought suddenly occurred to him. If the clock had been reset, then that meant that he still had his original birthday wish. He had one more chance to make the wish that he so desperately wanted to make. Hope flared for an instant inside of his chest. This was a wish that he was entitled to. He wouldn't be taking any wishes from anybody else. This was his very own, and he knew how to follow the rules to make it come true.

With his hand trembling slightly, he lit the match.

There was a soft knock on the door. Ben stood and moved to it.

He opened the door slowly and peered out.

"Mom?"

His expression fell when he saw that it was not his parents, but Candlewick that stood before him, his bowler hat in his hands.

I should have known. After all, I didn't have time to make my last wish, anyway.

But knowing and hoping are two separate things, Ben realized. And he had hoped to see his parents again.

"Oh. It's you. I thought . . ."

But he never finished the sentence. Ben moved back to the cot and sat down dejectedly. Candlewick followed, sitting next to him, a thoughtful expression on his face.

They sat in silence for a moment, each lost in thought. Finally, Candlewick broke the silence, staring at the corner of the room.

"You know, even if you had done it, it wouldn't have worked."

Ben didn't look up.

"There are some wishes that the Factory cannot make happen, and that is one of them. I would know. I tried it once myself when I was just about your age."

Ben's eyes glistened as he stared at the floor.

After a few minutes of silence, Ben spoke.

"I miss them so much."

"I understand."

Candlewick put a sympathetic arm around the boy. They sat there quietly for a while, Candlewick taking care not to make mention of the tears that Ben self-consciously wiped from his eyes.

Eventually, Candlewick broke the awkward silence.

"So, how do you feel about returning to the orphanage?"

Ben wiped a sleeve across his eyes and snorted. "I think I can handle it now."

Candlewick nodded. "I'm sure you can. No doubt about it, you've certainly proved that you can handle yourself. It's just that, well, there's an opening at the Factory now that I've been promoted, and I thought you might be interested in staying up at Wishworks with me."

Ben looked up, his eyes shining with hope. "Do you really mean it?"

Candlewick cleared his throat. "Well, you would need a little instruction on how to run the Kids' Birthday Wishes department, but I'm sure Perkins could give you a hand with that . . ."

He almost fell over sideways under the impact as Ben threw his arms around him. Chuckling, he hugged the small boy back.

"I guess that means you accept the job?"

Ben loosed his grip and nodded happily. "Thank you so much!"

Candlewick beamed at him as they stood up. "Of course."

Candlewick opened his magic pocket watch and smiled down at Ben.

"Ready?"

Ben noticed Rags laying on an old towel near his feet. The puppy let out a small whimper.

"Can Rags come, too?" Ben asked, hating to leave his best friend at the orphanage.

Candlewick nodded and Ben scooped the wriggling puppy into his arms.

There was the familiar flash of golden light as they were transported away from Pinch's Home for Wayward Boys forever.

Ben grinned from ear to ear as he stared at the familiar gates stretching upward before him. Rags barked excitedly and ran in circles on the wide lawn. A sudden thought occurred to Ben as he gazed at the immense factory.

"Um, Thom? Is it okay if I make my birthday wish now?"

Candlewick looked at him thoughtfully, then decided to honor Ben's request. He reached into his pocket and pulled out his watch.

There was a tiny flash of gold, and then a cupcake with a glowing candle appeared in Ben's hand.

Ben concentrated with his eyes closed. Then, with a single well-aimed puff, he blew out the candle.

A moment later, a huge grin spread across his face.

"So, what did you wish for?"

Candlewick gazed down at Ben, filled with curiosity.

Ben called to Rags, who dashed forward and leaped into his arms. He looked up at Candlewick with an expression of mock seriousness.

"Do you really think I'm that stupid?"

Candlewick laughed, and after removing his blue derby, shoved it down playfully on Ben's head. Ben grinned and after examining it for a moment handed it back.

"Thanks, but I think I'm gonna need to pick out one of my own—you know, find a uniform that fits my image. I'm

thinking maybe a really big top hat, the kind magicians wear. What do you think?"

Candlewick chuckled. "Sure, whatever you want. You're the boss."

What a great kid, Candlewick thought as they walked back to the towering spires. He opened the golden gates and watched Ben and Rags march happily through the entrance. *There is nothing I love more than making a kid's dream come true.*

Gazing at the numerous employees going about their daily activities, Ben realized that he was now a permanent part of this world. He, Benjamin Bartholomew Piff, had found a place for himself, a place where he was loved and needed. A place that he had never thought he would ever have again.

He whispered the words aloud that he had longed to hear himself say for longer than he could ever remember.

I'm home.

≋ *Appendix* ≋

A Timeline of Wishworks Presidents, Past to Present

1185–1200　　　**Cornelius Bubbdouble.**

　　　　　　　　Credited as the creator of the birthday
　　　　　　　　cake and candles.

1200–1235　　　**Wadsworth Pfefferminz.**

　　　　　　　　Originator of the Battlerang and failed
　　　　　　　　inventor of the heated back-scratcher.

1235–1310　　　**Wilbur Waffletoffee. Known as
　　　　　　　　"Wilbur the Ancient."**

　　　　　　　　Longest term as president in Wishworks
　　　　　　　　history.

1310–1347　　　**Ebenezer Hairyhead.**

　　　　　　　　Died in the Jinn rebellion.

1347–1490　　　**No president on record.**

1490–1526   Sephira Sparkletoe.

Credited with commissioning Leonardo da Vinci to design the Thaumaturgic Cardioscope. The Factory's effectiveness in granting wishes is tripled as a result.

1526–1527   Gimble Grimyfist.

Considered the worst president in Wishworks history. Impeached after one year in office.

1527–1606   Thaddeus Snooplewhoop.

Founder of the Snooplewhoop Everlasting Circus. Although credited with running the Factory, he spent most of his tenure in Leprechaun County entertaining the fair folk while his assistant, Pompo Poopypants, ran the Factory. Because of Pompo's ridiculous surname, most historians have left him out of the historical records. During his tenure, Pierre de Chaumpinon made his famous attempt to fly to the moon in a Funicula Chair.

1606–1633   **Socho Rumbleroot.**

1633–1678   **Percival "The Greedy" Pokenose.**
Convicted of spying for Curseworks.

1678–1724   **Wolfgang Warblegrunt.**
Founder of the Wishworks historical library and credited with uniting the Jinn empire by "destroying" all of the lamps that held them prisoner. To this day nobody knows if he succeeded in actually destroying them.

1724–1827   **Patrick McMurphy.**
The Factory's first leprechaun president.

1827–1898   **Bertram Snicklepants.**

1898–1912   **Penelope "Lucky Penny" Thicklepick.**
Considered by many to be the best president Wishworks has ever had. Responsible for Thomas Edison's creation of Wallace, Warren, and Wimbledon; fantastic pilot; and Battlerang expert.

1912–1952   **Finneas Cheeseweasle.**

President during the Great Wishworks War. Fought Abul-Cadabra and the evil Jinns and emerged victorious, destroying the Lamp of One Thousand Nightmares.

1952–2006   **Leonardo Snifflewiffle.**

2006–present   **Thomas Candlewick.**